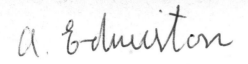

TWO THRILLERS

TWO THRILLERS

By

AGATHA CHRISTIE

AND

E. PHILLIPS OPPENHEIM

♠

THE WORLD'S GREATEST NEWSPAPER

DAILY EXPRESS FICTION LIBRARY

Printed in Great Britain

FOREWORD

FASHION in fiction changes from time to time in order to accommodate itself to the whims and fancies of the novel-reading public, but the fascination of the detective mystery story remains constant; and of all the various grades of novel-readers the devotees of the detective story are the most catholic—they include almost every possible type of reader. This form of fiction seems to appeal as strongly to the simple-minded citizen as to those possessed of the most brilliant brains—Judges, Philosophers, Scientists, Statesmen—in fact all sorts and conditions of deep thinkers seem to find relaxation in the "thriller."

These two crime stories, each with its tangled skein of mystery to unravel, are among the best that come from the pens of these two famous authors. And M. Poirot himself has now become a famous detective of fiction whose name will rank with that of Sherlock Holmes.

Agatha Christie's rise to fame was almost meteoric in its rapidity. In 1921 her first novel created a tremendous sensation, and was followed almost immediately by a series of striking successes. Then came the popular play *Alibi*, founded on her book, which was produced at the Haymarket Theatre, London, about eight years ago. Since then Mrs. Christie has gone from success to success, and to-day stands in the foremost rank of our novelists. Being interested in archeology, she has spent much time in the Middle East, and her excellent new novel, "Murder in Mesopotamia," in which Poirot appears once again, is the result of her sojourn in that part of the world.

Mr. E. Phillips Oppenheim, born in 1866, was educated at Wyggeston Grammar School, Leicester. He wrote his first story at the age of twenty, and since that time has averaged an output of two novels a year. He was the first writer to draw attention to the danger to peace in the arming of Germany in the years before 1914, and wrote no less than nine novels on this subject. He was of course, in consequence, put on the German black list. He is a story-teller pure and simple in contradistinction to the psychological novelist who is so prevalent to-day. Many of his stories have a delightful streak of humour running through them which adds enormously to their popularity, and his sales are enormous.

He is a keen sportsman, a confirmed golfer and a first-rate shot. He spends his time between England and the south of France at Cagnes-sur-Mer, where the late W. J. Locke was his near neighbour.

THE EDITOR.

THE UNDER DOG

THE UNDER DOG

CHAPTER I

LILY MARGRAVE smoothed her gloves out
on her knee with a nervous gesture, and
darted a glance at the occupant of the
big chair opposite her. She had heard
of M. Hercule Poirot, the well-known
investigator, but this was the first time
she had seen him in the flesh. The comic,
almost ridiculous aspect that he presented
disturbed her conception of him. Could
this funny little man, with the egg-shaped
head and the enormous moustaches, really
do the wonderful things that were claimed
for him? His occupation at the moment
struck her as particularly childish. He
was piling small blocks of coloured wood
one upon the other, and seemed far more
interested in the result than he was in the
story she was telling him.

At her sudden silence, however, he looked sharply across at her.

"Mademoiselle, continue, I pray of you. It is not that I do not attend. I attend very carefully, I assure you."

He began once more to pile the little blocks of wood one upon the other, while the girl's voice took up the tale again. It was a gruesome tale, a tale of violence and tragedy, but the girl's voice was so calm and unemotional, the recital was so concise and meticulous, that something of the savour of humanity seemed to have been left out of it.

She stopped at last.

"I hope," she said anxiously, "that I have made everything clear."

Poirot nodded his head several times in emphatic assent. Then he swept his hand across the wooden blocks, scattering them over the table, and leaning back in his chair, his finger tips pressed together and his eyes on the ceiling, he began to recapitulate.

"Sir Reuben Astwell was murdered ten days ago (that, of course, I already knew from the papers). On Wednesday, the day before yesterday, his nephew, M. Charles Leverson, was arrested by the police. The facts against him, as far as you know, are these (you will correct me if I am wrong, Mademoiselle): Sir Reuben was sitting up late, writing in his own special sanctum, the Tower room. Mr. Leverson came in late, letting himself in with a latch-key. He was overheard quarrelling with his uncle by the butler, whose room was directly below the Tower room. The quarrel ended with a sudden thud, as of a chair being thrown over, and a half-smothered cry. The butler was alarmed, and thought of getting up to see what was the matter, but as a few seconds later he heard Mr. Leverson leave the room whistling a tune gaily, he thought nothing more of it. On the following morning, however, a housemaid discovered Sir Reuben dead by his desk. He had been struck down by some heavy instrument. The butler, I gather, did not at once tell the story to the police. That was natural, I think, eh, Mademoiselle?"

The sudden question made Lily Margrave start.

"I beg your pardon?" she said vaguely.

"One looks for humanity in these matters, does one not?" said the little man. "As you recited the story to me—so admirably, so concisely—you made of the actors in the drama, machines—puppets. But me, I look always for human nature. I say to myself, this butler, this —what did you say his name was?"

"His name is Parsons," said Lily Margrave.

"This Parsons, then, he will have the characteristics of his class: he will object very strongly to the police, he will tell them as little as possible. Above all, he will say nothing that might seem to incriminate a member of the household. A house-breaker, a burglar—he will cling to that idea with all the strength of extreme obstinacy. Yes, the loyalties of the servant class are an extremely interesting study."

He leant back beaming, his finger-tips pressed together.

"In the meantime," he went on, "everyone in the household has told his or her tale, Mr. Leverson among the rest, and his tale was that he had come in late and gone up to bed without seeing his uncle."

"That is what he said," agreed Lily Margrave.

"And no one saw reason to doubt that tale," mused Poiret, "except, of course, Parsons. Then there comes down an inspector from Scotland Yard. Inspector Miller, you said, did you not? I know him. I have come across him once or twice in the past. He is what they call the sharp man, the ferret, the weasel— the much-praised individual who does not let the grass grow under his feet. Yes, I know him. And the sharp Inspector Miller, he sees what the local inspector has not seen—that Parsons is ill at ease and uncomfortable, and knows something that he has not told. *Eh bien!* he makes short work of Parsons. By now it has been clearly proved that no one broke into the house that night, that the murderer must be looked for inside the house and not outside. And Parsons is unhappy and frightened, and feels very relieved to have his secret knowledge drawn out of him. He has done his best to avoid scandal, but there are limits; and so Inspector Miller listens to Parsons's story, and asks a question or two, and then makes some private investigations of his own. The case he builds up is very strong—very strong indeed, Mademoiselle. Blood-stained fingers rested on the corner of the chest in the Tower room, and the finger-prints were those of Charles Leverson. The housemaid told him she emptied a basin of blood-stained water in Mr. Leverson's room the morning after the crime. He explained to her that he had cut his finger, and he *had* a little cut there; oh yes! but such a very little cut! The cuff of his evening-shirt had been washed, but they found blood-stains on the sleeve of his coat. He was hard pressed for money, and he inherited money at Sir Reuben's death. Oh yes, a very strong case, Mademoiselle"—he paused—"and yet you come to me to-day."

Lily Margrave shrugged her slender shoulders.

"As I told you, M. Poirot, Lady Astwell sent me."

"You would not have come of your own accord, eh?"

The little man glanced at her shrewdly. The girl did not answer.

"You do not reply to my question, Mademoiselle."

Lily Margrave began smoothing her gloves again.

"It is rather difficult for me, M. Poirot. I have my loyalty to Lady Astwell to consider. Strictly speaking, I am only her paid companion, but she has treated me more as though I were a daughter or a niece. She has been extraordinarily kind and, whatever her faults, I should not like to appear to criticize her actions, or—well—to prejudice you against taking up the case."

"Impossible to prejudice Hercule Poirot, *cela ne le fait pas*," declared the little man cheerily. "I perceive that you think Lady Astwell has in her bonnet the buzzing bee. Come now, is it not so?"

"If I must say——"

"Speak, Mademoiselle."

"I think the whole thing is simply silly."

"It strikes you like that, eh?"

"I don't want to say anything against Lady Astwell——"

She paused.

"I comprehend," murmured Poirot gently. "I comprehend perfectly."

His eyes invited her to go on. The girl yielded to his sympathetic and persuasive manner.

"She really is an awfully good sort, and frightfully kind, but she isn't—how can I put it? She isn't an educated woman. You know, she was an actress when Sir Reuben married her, and she has got all sorts of prejudices and superstitions. If she says a thing, it must be so, and she simply won't listen to reason. The inspector was not very tactful with her, and it put her back up. She says it is nonsense to suspect Mr. Leverson, and just the sort of stupid, pig-headed mistake the police would make, and that, of course, dear Charles did not do it."

"But she has no reasons, eh?"

"None whatever," said Miss Margrave very positively.

"Ah ha! is that so? Really now—well, I have met ladies like that before."

"I told her," said Lily, "that it would be no good coming to you with a mere statement like that and nothing to go on."

"You told her that," said Poirot; "did you really? That is interesting."

His eyes swept over Lily Margrave in a quick comprehensive survey, taking in the details of her neat, black tailor-made, the touch of white at her throat, an expensive crêpe-de-chine blouse showing dainty tucks, and the smart little black felt hat. He saw the elegance of her, the pretty face with its slightly pointed chin, and the dark-blue, long-lashed eyes. Insensibly his attitude changed; he was interested now, not so much in the case, as in the girl sitting opposite him.

"Lady Astwell is, I should imagine, Mademoiselle, just a trifle inclined to be unbalanced and hysterical?"

Lily Margrave nodded eagerly.

"That describes her exactly. She is, as I told you, very kind, but it is impossible to argue with her or to make her see things logically."

"Possibly she suspects someone on her own account," suggested Poirot; "someone quite absurd and impossible."

"That is exactly what she does do," cried Lily. "She has taken a great dislike to Sir Reuben's secretary, poor man. She says she *knows* he did it, and yet it has been proved quite conclusively that poor Mr. Trefusis cannot possibly have had anything to do with it."

"And she has no reasons?"

"Of course not; it is all intuition with her."

Lily Margrave's voice was very scornful.

"I perceive, Mademoiselle," said Poirot smiling, "that you do not believe in intuition?"

"I think it is nonsense," replied Lily frankly.

Poirot leaned back in his chair.

"*Les femmes*," he murmured, "they like to think that it is a special weapon that the good God has given them, and for every once that it shows them the truth, at least nine times it leads them astray."

"I know," said Lily; "but I have told you what Lady Astwell is like. You simply cannot argue with her."

"So you, Mademoiselle, being wise and discreet, came along to see me as you were bidden, and have managed to put me *au courant* of the situation."

Something in the tone of his voice made the girl look up sharply, but Hercule Poirot's gaze was fixed innocently upon the ceiling.

"Of course, I know," said Lily apologetically, "how very valuable your time is."

"You are too flattering, Mademoiselle," said Poirot; "but indeed—yes, it is true, at this present time I have many cases of moment on hand."

"I was afraid that might be so," said Lily rising. "I will tell Lady Astwell."

But Poirot did not rise also. Instead he lay back in his chair, and looked steadily up at the girl.

"You are in haste to be gone, Mademoiselle; sit down one more little moment, I pray of you."

He saw the colour flood into her face and ebb out again. She sat down once more, slowly and unwillingly.

"Mademoiselle is quick and decisive," said Poirot. "She must make allowances for an old man like myself, who comes to his decisions slowly. You mistook me, Mademoiselle. I did not say that I would not go down to Lady Astwell."

"You will come, then?"

The girl's tone was flat. She did not look at Poirot, but down at the ground, and so was unaware of the keen scrutiny with which he regarded her. At last he nodded his head as though replying to some question in his own mind.

"Tell Lady Astwell, Mademoiselle, that I am entirely at her service. I will be at—Mon Repos, is it not?—this afternoon."

He rose briskly to his feet. The girl followed suit.

"I—I will tell her. It is very good of you to come, M. Poirot. I am afraid, though, you will find you have been brought on a wild-goose chase."

"Very likely, but—who knows?"

He saw her out with punctilious courtesy to the door. Then he returned to the sitting-room, frowning, deep in thought. Once or twice he nodded his head. Then he opened the door of the bedroom adjoining, and called to his valet.

"My good George, prepare me, I pray of you, a little valise. I go down to the country this afternoon for several days."

"Very good, sir," said George.

He was an extremely English-looking person. Tall, cadaverous and unemotional.

"A young girl is a very interesting phenomenon, George," said Poirot, as he dropped once more into his arm-chair and lighted a cigarette. "Especially, you understand, when she has brains. To ask someone to do a thing and at the same time to put them against doing it, that is a delicate operation. It requires finesse. She was very adroit—oh! very adroit; but Hercule Poirot, my good George, is of a cleverness quite exceptional."

"I have heard you say so, sir," said George.

"It is not the secretary she has in mind," mused Poirot. "Lady Astwell's accusation of him she treats with contempt. All the same, she is anxious that no one should disturb the sleeping dogs. I, my good George, I go to disturb them. I go to make the dog fight. There is a drama there, at Mon Repos. A human drama, and it excites me. She was adroit, the little one, but not adroit enough. I wonder —I wonder what I shall find there?"

Into the dramatic pause which succeeded these words, George's voice broke apologetically.

"Shall I pack dress-clothes, sir?"

Poirot looked at him sadly, shaking his head.

"Always the concentration, the attention to your own job. You are very good for me, George. You are so exceedingly English."

CHAPTER II

WHEN the 4.55 drew up at Abbot's Cross station there descended from it M. Hercule Poirot, very neatly and foppishly attired, his moustaches waxed to a stiff point. He gave up his ticket, passed through the barrier, and was accosted by a tall chauffeur.

"Mr. Poirot?"

The little man beamed upon him.

"That is my name."

"This way, sir, if you please."

He held open the door of the big Rolls-Royce limousine. Poirot got in, and noted the luxury of the upholstery with approval.

The house was a bare three minutes from the station. The chauffeur descended once more and opened the door of the car, and Poirot stepped out. The butler was already holding the front door open. Poirot gave the outside of the house a

swift, appraising glance before passing
through the open door. It was a big,
solidly built, red-brick mansion, with no
pretensions to beauty, but with an air of
solid comfort. It stood quite near the
road, approached, as house agents are
wont to term it, by a short carriage-drive.
Four or five acres of garden stretched
away behind it. It was a house typical
of Abbot's Cross, which is fifty minutes by
rail from London, and scorns to call itself
a suburb.

Poirot stepped into the hall. The butler
relieved him deftly of his hat and over-
coat, then murmured with that deferential
undertone only to be achieved by the best
servants:

"Her Ladyship is expecting you, sir.
I was to take you to her as soon as you
arrived."

Poirot followed the butler up the soft
carpeted stairs. This, without doubt, was
Parsons, a very well trained servant, with
a manner suitably devoid of emotion.
At the top of the staircase he turned to
the right, along a corridor. He passed

through a door into a little anteroom, from which two more doors led. He threw open the left-hand of these, and announced:

"M. Poirot, milady."

The room was not a very large one, and it was crowded with furniture and knick-knacks. A woman, dressed in black, got up from a sofa by the fireplace, and came quickly towards Poirot. Lady Astwell was a big, highly-coloured woman. She retained traces of a past beauty of no mean order, but she was the kind who runs to fat, and she could hardly have weighed less than thirteen stone.

"M. Poirot," said Lady Astwell with out-stretched hand. Her eyes ran rapidly over the dandified figure. She paused a minute, ignoring the little man's bow over her hand, and his murmured "My Lady." And then, releasing his hand after a sudden, vigorous pressure, she exclaimed:

"I believe in small men! They are the clever ones."

"Inspector Miller," murmured Poirot, "is, I think, a tall man?"

"He is a bumptious idiot," said Lady

Astwell. "Sit down here by me, will you, M. Poirot?"

She indicated the sofa, and went on:

"Lily did her best to put me off sending for you, but I have not come to my time of life without knowing my own mind."

"A rare accomplishment," said Poirot, as he followed her to the settee.

Lady Astwell settled herself comfortably among the cushions and turned so as to face him. The light from the west window fell full on her face, with its high colour, its henna-red hair, and the eyes that were still dark blue and beautiful.

"Lily is a dear girl," said Lady Astwell, "but she thinks she knows everything and, as often as not, in my experience, those sort of people are wrong. I am not clever, M. Poirot; I never have been, but I am right where many a stupider person is wrong. I believe in *guidance*. Now do you want me to tell you who is the murderer, or do you not? A woman knows, M. Poirot."

"Does Miss Margrave know?" asked Poirot.

"What did she tell you?" asked Lady Astwell sharply.

"She gave me the facts of the case," said Poirot.

"The facts? Oh! of course they are dead against Charles, but I tell you, M. Poirot, he didn't do it. I know he didn't."

She bent upon him an earnestness that was almost disconcerting.

"You are very positive, Lady Astwell."

"Trefusis killed my husband, M. Poirot. I am sure of it."

"Why?"

"Why should he kill him, do you mean, or why am I sure? I tell you I know it. I am funny about those things, I make up my mind at once, and I stick to it."

"Did Mr. Trefusis benefit in any way by Sir Reuben's death?"

"Never left him a penny," returned Lady Astwell promptly. "Now that shows you dear Reuben can't have liked or trusted him."

"Had he been with Sir Reuben long, then?"

"Close on nine years."

"That is a long time," said Poirot softly: "a very long time to remain in the employment of one man. Yes, Mr. Trefusis, he must have known his employer well."

Lady Astwell stared at him.

"What are you driving at? I don't see what that has got to do with it."

"I was following out a little idea of my own," said Poirot. "A little idea—not interesting perhaps, but original—on the effects of service."

Lady Astwell still stared.

"You are very clever, aren't you?" she said in rather a doubtful tone. "Everybody says so."

Hercule Poirot laughed.

"Perhaps you shall pay me that compliment, too, Madame, one of these days. But let us return to the motive. Tell me, now, of your household, of the people who were here in the house on the day of the tragedy."

"There was Charles, of course," said Lady Astwell.

"He was your husband's nephew, I understand, not yours?"

"Yes; Charles was the only son of Reuben's sister. She married a comparatively rich man, but he came one of those crashes they do in the city, and he died and his wife, too, and Charles came to live with us. He was twenty-three at the time, and going to be a barrister. But when the trouble came, Reuben took him into his office."

"He was industrious—Mr. Charles?" hinted Poirot.

"I like a man who is quick in the up-take," said Lady Astwell with a nod of approval. "No; that's just the trouble, Charles was *not* industrious. He was always having rows with his uncle over some muddle or other that he had made. Not that poor Reuben was an easy man to get on with. Many's the time I've told him that he had forgotten what it was to be young himself. He was very different in those days, M. Poirot."

Lady Astwell heaved a sigh of reminiscence.

"When I think of that time in Manchester when he first saw me. You know I was in the chorus of the pantomime then. Ah, yes; very different in those days." She sighed again.

"Changes must come, Milady," said Poirot. "It is the law."

"Still," said Lady Astwell, "he was never really rude to *me*—at least, if he was, he was always sorry afterwards—poor dear Reuben."

"He was difficult, eh?" said Poirot.

"*I* could always manage him," said Lady Astwell, with the air of a successful lion-tamer; "but it was rather awkward sometimes when he would lose his temper with the servants. There are ways of doing it, you know, and Reuben's was not the right way."

"How exactly did Sir Reuben leave his money, Lady Astwell?"

"Half to me and half to Charles," replied Lady Astwell promptly. "The lawyers don't put it simply like that, of course, but that's what it amounts to."

Poirot nodded his head thoughtfully.

"I see—I see," he murmured. "Now, Lady Astwell, I will demand of you that you will describe to me the household. There was yourself, and Sir Reuben's nephew, Mr. Charles Leverson, and the secretary, Mr. Owen Trefusis, and there was Miss Lily Margrave. Perhaps you will tell me something of that young lady."

"You want to know about Lily?"

"Yes. She has been with you long?"

"About a year. I have had a lot of secretary-companions, you know, but somehow or other they have all got on my nerves. Lily was different. She was tactful and full of commonsense, and besides, she looks so nice. I do like to have a pretty face about me, M. Poirot. I am a funny kind of person, I take likes and dislikes straight away. As soon as I saw that girl I said to myself, 'she'll do.'"

"Did she come to you through friends, Lady Astwell?"

"I think she answered an advertisement. Yes—that was it."

"You know something of her people, of where she comes from?"

"Her father and mother are out in India, I believe. I don't really know much about them; but you can see at a glance that Lily is a lady, can't you, M. Poirot?"

"Oh, perfectly, perfectly!"

"Of course," went on Lady Astwell, "I am not a lady myself. I know it, and the servants know it; but there is nothing mean-spirited about me. I can appreciate the real thing when I see it, and no one could be nicer than Lily has been to me. I look upon that girl almost as a daughter, M. Poirot, indeed I do."

Poirot's right hand strayed out and straightened one or two of the objects lying on a little table near him.

"Did Sir Reuben share this feeling?" he asked.

His eyes were on the knick-knacks, but doubtless he noted the pause before Lady Astwell's answer came.

"With a man it's different. Of course, they—they got on very well together."

"Thank you, Madame," said Poirot. He was smiling to himself.

"And these were the only people in the

house that night," he asked, "excepting, of course, the servants?"

"Oh, there was Victor," said Lady Astwell.

"Victor?"

"Yes, my husband's brother. you know, and his partner."

"He lived with you?"

"No; he had just arrived on a visit. He has been out in West Africa for the last four years."

"West Africa," murmured Poirot reflectively.

He had learned that Lady Astwell could be trusted to develop a subject herself, if sufficient time was given her.

"They say it's a wonderful country; but *I* think it's the kind of place that has a very bad effect upon a man. They drink too much, and they get uncontrolled. None of the Astwells have good tempers, and Victor's since he came back from Africa has been simply too shocking. He has frightened *me* once or twice."

"Did he frighten Miss Margrave, I wonder?" murmured Poirot gently,

"Lily? Oh, I don't think he has seen much of Lily."

Poirot made a note or two in a diminutive note-book, then he put the pencil back in its loop and returned the note-book to his pocket as he rose to his feet.

"I thank you, Lady Astwell. I will now, if I may, interview the good Parsons."

"Will you have him up here?"

Lady Astwell's hand moved towards the bell. Poirot arrested the gesture quickly.

"No, no, a thousand times no. I will descend to him."

"If you think it is better——"

Lady Astwell was clearly disappointed at not being able to participate in the forthcoming scene. Poirot adopted an air of mysterious secrecy.

"It is essential," he hissed, and left Lady Astwell duly impressed.

He found Parsons in the butler's pantry, polishing silver. Poirot opened the proceedings with one of his funny little bows.

"I must explain myself," he said. "I am a detective agent."

"Yes, sir," said Parsons; "we gathered as much."

His tone was respectful but aloof.

"Lady Astwell sent for me," continued Poirot. "She is not satisfied; no, she is not satisfied at all."

"I have heard her Ladyship say so on several occasions," said Parsons.

"In fact," said Poirot, "I recount to you the things you already know? Eh? Let us then not waste time on these bagatelles. Take me, if you will be so good, to your bedroom, and tell me exactly what it was you heard there on the night of the murder."

The butler's room was on the ground floor, adjoining the servants' hall. It had barred windows, and the strong room was in one corner of it. Parsons indicated the narrow bed with an unconsciously dramatic gesture.

"I had retired, sir, at eleven o'clock. Miss Margrave had gone to bed, and Lady Astwell was with Sir Reuben in the Tower room."

"Lady Astwell was with Sir Reuben? Ah! proceed."

"The Tower room, sir, is directly over this. If people are talking in it one can hear the murmur of voices, but naturally not anything that is said. I must have fallen asleep about half-past eleven. It was full on twelve o'clock when I was awakened by the sound of the front door being slammed to, and knew Mr. Leverson had returned. Presently I heard footsteps overhead, and a minute or two later Mr. Leverson's voice talking to Sir Reuben. It was my fancy at the time, sir, that Mr. Leverson was—I should not exactly like to say drunk, but inclined to be a little indiscreet and noisy. He was shouting at his uncle at the top of his voice. I caught a word or two here or there, but not enough to understand what it was all about, and then there was a sharp cry, a sort of yell more than anything else, and a heavy thud."

There was a pause, and Parsons repeated the last words in evident self-approval.

"A heavy thud," he said impressively.

"If I mistake not, it is a *dull* thud in most works of romance," murmured Poirot.

"Maybe, sir," said Parsons severely. "It was a *heavy* thud I heard."

"A thousand pardons," said Poirot.

"Do not mention it, sir. After the thud, in the silence, I heard Mr. Leverson's voice, as plain as plain can be, raised high. 'My God,' he said, 'My God,' just like that, sir."

Parsons, from his first reluctance to tell the tale, had now progressed to a thorough enjoyment of it. He fancied himself mightily as a narrator. Poirot played up to him.

"*Mon Dieu!*" he murmured. "What emotion you must have experienced!"

"Yes, indeed, sir," said Parsons, "as you say, sir. Not that I thought very much of it at the time. But it *did* occur to me to wonder if anything was amiss, and whether I had better go up and see. I went to turn the electric light on, and was unfortunate enough to knock over a chair. To tell you the truth, I barked my shins on it pretty severely. I opened the door and went through the servants' hall, and opened the other door which gives on a passage. The back stairs lead up from there, and as I stood at the bottom of them hesitating, I heard Mr. Leverson's voice from up above, speaking hearty and cheery-like. 'No harm done, luckily,' he says. 'Good night,' and I heard him move off along the passage to his own room whistling cheerily. Of course, I went back to bed at once. Just something knocked over, that's all I thought it was. I ask you, sir, was I to think Sir Reuben was murdered, with Mr. Leverson saying good night and all?"

"You are sure it was Mr. Leverson's voice you heard?"

Parsons looked at him pityingly, and Poirot saw clearly enough that, right or wrong, Parsons's mind was made up on this point.

"Is there anything further you would like to ask me, sir?"

"There is one thing," said Poirot; "do you like Mr. Leverson?"

"I—I beg your pardon, sir?"

"It is a simple question. Do you like Mr. Leverson?"

Parsons, from being startled at first, now seemed embarrassed.

"The general opinion in the servants' hall, sir——" he said, and paused.

"By all means," said Poirot; "put it that way if it pleases you."

"The opinion is, sir, that Mr. Leverson is an open-handed young gentleman, but not, if I may say so, particularly intelligent, sir."

"Ah!" said Poirot. "Do you know, Parsons, that without having seen him, that is also precisely my opinion of Mr. Leverson?"

"Indeed, sir."

"What is your opinion—I beg your pardon—the opinion of the servants' hall, of the secretary, M. Trefusis?"

"He is a very quiet, patient gentleman, sir. Anxious to give no trouble."

"*Vraiment*," said Poirot.

The butler coughed.

"Her Ladyship, sir," he murmured, "is apt to be a little hasty in her judgments."

"Then, in the opinion of the servants' hall, Mr. Leverson committed the crime?"

"We none of us wish to think it was Mr. Leverson," said Parsons, with a touch of eagerness in his manner. "I am sure I kept quiet about what I heard as long as I could. We—well, plainly, we didn't think Mr. Leverson had it in him, sir."

"But he has a somewhat violent temper, has he not?" asked Poirot.

Parsons came nearer to him and lowered his voice.

"If you are asking me who had the most violent temper in the house——"

Poirot held up a hand to arrest him.

"Ah! but that is not the question I should ask," he said softly. "My question would be, who has the best temper?"

Parsons stared at him open-mouthed.

CHAPTER III

It has been said of Hercule Poirot that he took a distinct pleasure in mystifying people. He has been accused of deliberately wrapping up his meaning in obscure sentences. In this case he noted with satisfaction that Parsons's mouth remained open, and that an expression of utter bewilderment rested on the butler's countenance. Poirot wasted no further time on him. With an amiable little bow—he was always amiable—he left the room and wandered out into the big square hall of Mon Repos. There he stood a minute or two in thought; then, at a slight sound that came to him, cocked his head on one side in the manner of a perky robin, and finally, with noiseless steps, crossed to one of the doors that led out of the hall. He stood in the doorway, looking into the room: it was a small room furnished as a library. At a big desk at the further end of it, sat a thin, pale young man busily writing. He had a receding chin, and wore pince-nez.

Poirot watched him for some minutes, and then he broke the silence by giving a completely artificial and theatrical cough.

"Ahem!" coughed M. Hercule Poirot.

The young man at the desk stopped writing, and turned his head. He did not appear unduly startled, but an expression of perplexity gathered on his face as he eyed Poirot.

The latter came forward with a little bow.

"I have the honour of speaking to Mr. Trefusis, yes? Ah! my name is Poirot, Hercule Poirot. You may, perhaps, have heard of me?"

"Oh!—er—yes, certainly," said the young man.

Poirot eyed him attentively. Owen Trefusis was about thirty-three years of age, and the detective saw at once why nobody was inclined to treat Lady Astwell's accusation seriously. Mr. Owen Trefusis was a prim, proper young man, disarmingly meek, the type of man who can be, and is, systematically bullied. One could feel quite sure that he would never display resentment.

"Lady Astwell sent for you, of course," said the secretary. "She mentioned that she was going to do so. Is there any way in which I can help you?"

His manner was polite without being effusive. Poirot accepted a chair, and murmured gently.

"Has Lady Astwell said anything to you of her beliefs and suspicions?"

Owen Trefusis smiled a little.

"As far as that goes," he said, "I believe she suspects me. It is absurd, but there it is. She has hardly spoken a civil word to me since, and she shrinks against the wall as I pass by in the most approved melodramatic fashion."

His manner was perfectly natural, and there was more amusement than resentment in his voice. Poirot nodded with an air of engaging frankness.

"Between ourselves," he explained, "she said the same thing to me. I did not argue with her—me, I have made it a rule never to argue with very positive ladies. You comprehend, it is a waste of time."

"Oh, quite."

"I say 'Yes, milady'—'Oh, perfectly, milady'—'*Precisément*, milady.' They mean nothing, those words, but they soothe all the same. I make my investigations, for though it seems almost impossible that anyone except Mr. Leverson could have committed the crime, yet—well, the impossible has happened before now."

"I understand your position perfectly," said the secretary. "Please regard me as entirely at your service."

"*Bon*," said Poirot; "we understand one another. Now recount to me the events of that evening. Better start with dinner."

"Leverson was not at dinner, as you doubtless know," said the secretary. "He had a serious disagreement with his uncle, and went off to dine at the Golf Club. Sir Reuben was in a very bad temper in consequence."

"Not too amiable, *le Monsieur*, eh?" hinted Poirot delicately.

Trefusis laughed.

"Oh! he was a tartar! I haven't worked with him for nine years without knowing most of his little ways. He was an extraordinarily difficult man, M. Poirot. He would get into childish fits of rage and abuse anybody who came near him. I was used to it by that time; I had got into the habit of paying absolutely no attention to anything he said. He was not bad-hearted really, but he could be most foolish and exasperating in his manner. The great thing was never to answer him back."

"Were other people as wise as you were in that respect?"

Trefusis shrugged his shoulders.

"Lady Astwell enjoyed a good row," he said. "She was not in the least afraid of Sir Reuben, and she always stood up to him, and gave him as good as she got. They always made it up afterwards, and Sir Reuben was really devoted to her."

"Did they quarrel that last night?" asked Poirot suddenly.

The secretary looked at him sideways, and hesitated a minute; then:

"I believe so," he said. "What made you ask?"

"An idea, that is all."

"I don't know, of course," explained the secretary; "but things looked as though they were working up that way. I know the signs pretty well by now."

Poirot did not pursue the topic.

"Who else was at dinner?"

"Miss Margrave, Mr. Victor Astwell and myself."

"And afterwards?"

"We went into the drawing-room. Sir Reuben did not accompany us. About ten minutes later he came in and hauled me over the coals for some trifling matter about a letter. I went up with him to the Tower room and set the thing straight. Then Mr. Victor Astwell came in and said he had something he wished to talk to his brother about, so I went downstairs and joined the two ladies. About a quarter of an hour later, I heard Sir Reuben's bell ringing violently, and Parsons came to say I was to go up to Sir Reuben at once. As I entered the room, Mr. Victor Astwell was coming out; he nearly knocked me over. Something had evidently happened to upset him—he has a very violent temper. I really believe he didn't see me."

"Did Sir Reuben make any comment on the matter?"

"He said, 'Victor is a lunatic; he will do for somebody some day when he is in one of these rages.'"

"Ah!" said Poirot. "Have you any idea what the trouble was about?"

"I couldn't say at all."

Poirot turned his head very slowly and looked at the secretary. Those last words had been uttered too hastily. He formed the conviction that Trefusis could have said more had he wished to do so. But once again Poirot did not press the question.

"And then? Proceed, I pray of you."

"I worked with Sir Reuben for about an hour and a half. At eleven o'clock Lady Astwell came in, and Sir Reuben told me I could go to bed."

"And you went?"

"Yes."

"Have you any idea how long she stayed with him?"

"None at all. Her room is on the first floor, and mine is on the second, so I should not hear her go to bed in any case."

"I see."

Poirot nodded his head once or twice, and sprang to his feet.

"And now, monsieur, take me to the Tower room."

He followed the secretary up the broad stairs to the first landing. Here Trefusis led him along the corridor, and through a baize door at the end of it which gave on the servants' staircase and on a short passage that ended in a door. They passed through this door and found themselves on the scene of the crime.

It was a lofty room, twice as high as any of the others, and was roughly about thirty feet square. Swords and assegais adorned the walls, and many native curios were arranged about on tables. At the far end, in the embrasure of the window, was a large writing-table. Poirot crossed straight to it.

"It was here Sir Reuben was found, eh?"
Trefusis nodded.

"He was struck from behind, I understand?"

Again the secretary nodded.

"The crime was committed with one of these native clubs," he explained. "A tremendously heavy thing. Death must have been practically instantaneous."

"That strengthens the conviction that the crime was not premeditated. A sharp quarrel, and a weapon snatched up almost unconsciously."

"Yes; it does not look well for poor Leverson."

"And the body was found fallen forwards on the desk?"

"No; it had slipped sideways to the ground."

"Ah!" said Poirot; "it is curious, that."

"Why curious?" asked the secretary sharply.

"Because of this."

Poirot pointed to a round, irregular stain on the polished surface of the writing-table.

"That is a blood-stain, *mon ami*," he said, nodding his head sagely.

"It may have splattered there," suggested Trefusis; "or it may have been made later, when they moved the body."

"Very possibly, very possibly," said the little man. "There is only the one door to this room?"

"There is a staircase here."

Trefusis pulled aside a velvet curtain in the corner of the room nearest the door, where a small spiral staircase led upwards.

"This place was originally built by an astronomer. The stairs lead up to the tower where the telescope was fixed. Sir Reuben had the place fitted up as a bedroom, and sometimes slept there if he was working very late."

Poirot went nimbly up the steps. The circular room upstairs was plainly furnished with a camp bed, a chair and dressing-table. Poirot satisfied himself that there was no other exit, and then came down again to where Trefusis stood waiting for him.

"Did you hear Mr. Leverson come in?" he asked.

Trefusis shook his head.

"I was fast asleep by that time."

Poirot nodded. He looked slowly round the room.

"*Eh bien!*" he said at last. "I do not think there is anything further here, unless—perhaps you would be so kind as to draw the curtains for a moment."

Obediently Trefusis pulled the heavy black curtains across the window at the far end of the room. Poirot switched on the light, which was masked by a big alabaster bowl hanging from the ceiling.

"There was a desk light, eh?" he asked.

For reply the secretary switched on a powerful, green-shaded hand-lamp, which stood on the writing-table. Poirot switched the other light off, then on, then off again. Finally, he grunted approval.

"*C'est bien!* I have finished here."

He passed out of the room.

"Dinner is at half-past seven," murmured the secretary.

"I thank you, Mr. Trefusis, for your many amiabilities."

"Not at all."

Poirot went thoughtfully along the corridor to the room appointed for him. The immovable George was there laying out his master's dress things. Poirot sat down in an arm-chair in front of the fire.

"My good George," he said presently, "I shall, I hope, meet at dinner a certain gentleman who begins to intrigue me greatly. A man who has come home from the tropics, George. With a tropical temper—so it is said. A man whom Parsons tries to tell me about, and whom Lily Margrave does not mention. The late Sir Reuben had a temper of his own, George. Supposing such a man to come into contact with a man whose temper was worse than his own—how do you say it? The fur would jump about, eh?"

"'Would fly' is the correct expression, sir; and it is not always the case, sir, not by a long way."

"No?"

Poirot's tone was encouraging.

"No, sir. There was my Aunt Jemima, sir; a most shrewish tongue she had, bullied a poor sister of hers who lived with her something shocking she did. Nearly worried the life out of her. But if anyone came along who stood up to her, well, it was a very different thing. It was meekness she couldn't a'bear."

"Ha!" said Poirot; "it is suggestive—that."

George coughed apologetically.

"Is there anything I can do in any way," he inquired delicately, "to—er—assist you, sir?"

"Certainly," said Poirot promptly. "You can find out for me what coloured evening-dress Miss Lily Margrave wore that night, and which housemaid attends on her."

George received these commands with his usual:

"Very good, sir; I will have the information for you in the morning."

Poirot rose from his seat and stood gazing into the fire, while George relieved him dexterously of his coat.

"You are very useful to me, George," he murmured. "Do you know, I shall not forget your Aunt Jemima."

CHAPTER IV

POIROT did not, after all, see Victor Astwell that night. A telephone message came from him that he was detained in London.

"He attends to the affairs of your late husband's business, eh?" asked Poirot of Lady Astwell.

"Victor is a partner," she explained. "He went out to Africa to look into some mining concessions for the firm. It *was* mining, wasn't it, Lily?"

"Yes, Lady Astwell."

"Gold mines, I think; or was it copper or tin? You ought to know, Lily, you were always asking Reuben questions about it all. Oh! do be careful, dear, you will have that vase over."

"It is dreadfully hot in here with the fire," said the girl. "Shall I—shall I open the window a little?"

"If you like, dear," said Lady Astwell placidly. "I'm much too fond of a froust myself, I know."

Poirot watched while the girl went across to the window and opened it. She stood there a minute or two breathing in the cool night air. When she returned and sat down in her seat, Poirot said to her politely:

"So Mademoiselle is interested in mines?"

"Oh, not really," said the girl indifferently. "I listened to Sir Reuben; but I don't know anything about the subject."

"You pretended very well then," said Lady Astwell. "Poor Reuben actually thought you had some ulterior motive in asking him all those questions."

The little detective's eyes had not moved from the fire, into which he was steadily staring, but nevertheless, he did not miss the quick flush of vexation on Lily Margrave's face. Very tactfully, he changed the conversation. When the hour for "Good nights" came, Poirot said to his hostess:

"May I have just two little words with you, madame?"

Lily Margrave vanished discreetly. Lady Astwell looked inquiringly at the detective.

"You were the last person to see Sir Reuben alive that night, Lady Astwell?"

She nodded. Tears sprang into her eyes, and she hastily held a black-edged handkerchief to them.

"Ah! do not distress yourself. I beg of you, do not distress yourself."

"It's all very well, M. Poirot, but I can't help it."

"I am a triple imbecile thus to vex you."

"No, no; go on. What were you going to say?"

"It was about eleven o'clock, I fancy, when you went into the Tower room, and Sir Reuben dismissed Mr. Trefusis. Is that right?"

"It must have been about then," she agreed.

"How long were you with him?"

"It was just a quarter to twelve when I got up to my room. I remember glancing at the clock on my mantelpiece——"

"Lady Astwell, will you tell me what your conversation with your husband was about?"

Lady Astwell sank down on the sofa and broke down completely. Her sobs were vigorous and convincing.

"We — qua — qua — quarrelled," she moaned.

"What about?" Poirot's voice was coaxing, almost tender.

"L—l—lots of things. It b-b-began with L-Lily. Reuben took a dislike to her— for no reason, and said he had caught her interfering with his papers. He wanted to send her away, and I said she was a dear girl, and I would not have it. And then he s-s-started shouting me down, and I wouldn't have that, so I just told him what I thought of him. Not that I really meant it, M. Poirot, and he said he had taken me out of the gutter to marry me, and I said——Oh, but what does it all matter now? I shall never forgive myself. You know how it is, M. Poirot. I always did say a good row clears the air, and how was I to know someone was going to murder him that very night? Poor old Reuben——

with the best heart in the world underneath
his spoilt-child ways."

Poirot had listened sympathetically to
all this outburst. At intervals he had
interposed soothing murmurs. Now, as
Lady Astwell wiped her eyes and turned
her swollen face towards him, he took her
hand and patted it gently.

"I have caused you suffering," he said.
"I apologize. Let us now be very business-
like—very practical, very exact. You still
cling to your idea that Mr. Trefusis murdered your husband?"

Lady Astwell drew herself up.

"A woman's instinct, M. Poirot," she
said solemnly, "never lies."

"Exactly, exactly," said Poirot. "But
when did he do it?"

"When? After I left him, of course."

"You left Sir Reuben at a quarter to
twelve. At five minutes to twelve Mr.
Leverson came in. In that ten minutes
you say the secretary came down from his
bedroom and murdered him?"

"It is perfectly possible," said Lady
Astwell.

"So many things are possible," said Poirot. "It could be done in ten minutes. Oh, yes! But was it?"

"Of course, he *says* he was in bed and fast asleep," said Lady Astwell; "but who is to know if he was or not?"

"Nobody saw him about," Poirot reminded her.

"Everybody was in bed and fast asleep," said Lady Astwell triumphantly. "Of course nobody saw him."

"I wonder," said Poirot to himself, very softly. "Yes, I wonder.

"*Eh bien!* Lady Astwell—I will wish you good night."

CHAPTER V

GEORGE deposited a tray of early-morning coffee by his master's bedside.

"Miss Margrave, sir, wore a dress of light-green chiffon on the night in question."

"Thank you, George; you are most reliable."

"The third housemaid looks after Miss Margrave, sir. Her name is Gladys."

"Thank you, George. You are quite invaluable."

"Not at all, sir."

"It is a fine morning," said Poirot, looking out of the window, "and no one is likely to be astir very early. I think, my good George, that we shall have the Tower room to ourselves if we proceed there to make a little experiment."

"You need me, sir?"

"The experiment," said Poirot, "will not be painful."

The curtains were still drawn in the Tower room when they arrived there. George was about to pull them, when Poirot restrained him.

"We will leave the room as it is. Just turn on the desk lamp."

The valet obeyed.

"Now, my good George, sit down in that chair. Dispose yourself as though you were writing. *Très bien!* Me, I seize a club, I steal up behind you, so, and I hit you on the back of the head."

"Yes, sir," said George.

"Ah!" said Poirot; "but when I hit you, do not continue to write. You comprehend, I cannot be exact. I cannot hit you with the same force with which the assassin hit Sir Reuben. When it comes to that point we must do the make-believe. I hit you on the head, and you collapse, so. The arms well relaxed, the body limp. Permit me to arrange you. But no, do not flex your muscles."

He heaved a sigh of exasperation.

"You press admirably the trousers, George," he said, "but the imagination you possess it not. Get up and let me take your place."

Poirot in his turn sat down at the writing-table.

"I write"—he declared—"I write busily. You steal up behind me, you hit me on the head with the club. Crash! The pen slips from my fingers, I drop forward, but not very far forward for the chair is low, and the desk is high, and moreover my arms support me. Have the goodness, George, to go back to the door, stand there, and tell me what you see."

"Ahem!"

"Yes, George?" encouragingly.

"I see you, sir, sitting at the desk."

"*Sitting* at the desk?"

"It is a little difficult to see plainly, sir," explained George, "being such a long way away, sir, and the lamp being heavily shaded. If I might turn on this light, sir?"

His hand reached out to the switch.

"Not at all," said Poirot sharply. "We shall do very well as we are. Here am I bending over the desk, there are you standing by the door. Advance now,

George; advance and put your hand on my shoulder."

George obeyed.

"Lean on me a little, George, to steady yourself on your feet as it were. Ah! *Voila!*"

Hercule Poirot's limp body slid artistically sideways.

"I collapse—so!" he observed. "Yes; it is very well imagined. There is now something most important that must be done."

"Indeed, sir?" said the valet.

"Yes, it is necessary that I should breakfast well."

The little man laughed heartily at his own joke.

"The stomach, George, it must not be ignored."

George maintained a disapproving silence. Poirot went downstairs chuckling happily to himself. He was pleased at the way things were shaping. After breakfast he made the acquaintance of Gladys, the third housemaid. He was very interested in what she could tell him of the crime. She was sympathetic towards Charles, although she had no doubt of his guilt.

"Poor young gentleman, sir, it seems hard, it does, him not being quite himself at the time."

"He and Miss Margrave should have got on well together," suggested Poirot, "as the only two young people in the house."

Gladys shook her head.

"Very stand-offish, Miss Lily was with him. She wouldn't have no carryings-on, and she made it plain."

"He was fond of her, was he, eh, Mademoiselle Gladys?"

"Oh, only in passing, so to speak; no harm in it, sir. Mr. Victor Astwell, now he *is* properly gone on Miss Lily."

She giggled.

"Ah! *Vraiment!*"

Gladys giggled again.

"Sweet on her straight away he was. Of course, coming from Africa with all those ugly black creatures, it is no wonder he was struck. Miss Lily is just like a lily, isn't she, sir? So tall and such a lovely shade of gold hair."

"She should wear a green evening frock," mused Poirot. "There is a certain shade of green——"

"She has one, sir," said Gladys eagerly. "Of course, she can't wear it now, being in mourning, but she had it on the very night Sir Reuben died."

"It should be a light green, not a dark green," said Poirot.

"It is a light green, sir. If you wait a minute I'll show it to you. Miss Lily has just gone out with the dogs."

Poirot nodded. He knew that as well as Gladys did; in fact it was only after seeing Lily safely off the premises, that he had gone in search of the housemaid. Gladys hurried away, and returned a few minutes later with a green evening dress on a hanger.

"*Exquis!*" murmured Poirot holding up hands of admiration. "Permit me to take it to the light a minute."

He took the dress from Gladys, turned his back on her and hurried to the window. He bent over it, then held it out at arm's length.

"It is perfect," he declared. "Perfectly

ravishing. A thousand thanks for showing it to me."

"Not at all, sir," said Gladys. "We all know that Frenchmen are interested in ladies' dresses."

"You are too kind," murmured Poirot.

He watched her hurry away again with the dress. Then he looked down at his two hands and smiled. In the right hand was a tiny pair of nail scissors; in the left was a neatly clipped fragment of green chiffon.

"And now," he murmured, "to be heroic."

He returned to his own apartment and summoned George.

"On the dressing-table, my good George, you will perceive a gold scarf-pin."

"Yes, sir."

"On the wash-stand is a solution of carbolic. Immerse, I pray you, the point of the pin in the carbolic."

George did as he was bid. He had long ago ceased to wonder at the vagaries of his master.

"I have done that, sir."

"*Très bien!* Now approach. I tender

to you my first finger; insert the point of the pin in it if you will be so good."

"Excuse me, sir, you want me **to** prick you, sir?"

"But yes, you have guessed correctly. You must draw blood, you understand, George; but not too much. A nicely regulated prick."

George took hold of his master's finger. Poirot shut his eyes, and leaned back. The valet stabbed at the finger with the scarf-pin, and Poirot uttered a shrill yell.

"*Je vous remercie*, George," he said. "What you have done is ample, ample."

Taking a small piece of green chiffon from his pocket, he dabbed his finger with it gingerly.

"The operation has succeeded to a miracle," he remarked, gazing at the result. "You have no curiosity, George? Now that is admirable."

The valet had just taken a discreet look out of the window.

"Excuse me, sir," he murmured, "a gentleman has driven up in a large car."

"Ah! ah!" said Poirot. He rose briskly

to his feet. "The elusive Mr. Victor Astwell. I go down to make his acquaintance."

Poirot was destined to hear Mr. Victor Astwell some time before he saw him. A loud voice rang out from the hall.

"Mind what you are doing, you damned idiot. That case has got glass in it. Curse you, Parsons, get out of the way. Put it down you b—— fool."

Poirot skipped nimbly down the stairs. Victor Astwell was a big man, broad of shoulder, with a bronzed, square-cut face, not unattractive. Poirot bowed to him politely.

"Who the devil are you?" roared the big man.

Poirot bowed again.

"My name, Monsieur, is Hercule Poirot."

"Lord!" said Victor Astwell. "So Nancy sent for you after all, did she? Come in here."

He put a hand on Poirot's shoulder and steered him into the library.

"So you are the fellow they make such a fuss about," he remarked, looking him up and down. "Sorry for my language just now. That chauffeur of mine is a damned ass, and Parsons always does get on my nerves, blithering old idiot."

He went over to a side table on which was a decanter, and a couple of soda-water syphons. Poirot declined his silent invitation, and he helped himself to a stiff whisky-and-soda.

"I don't suffer fools gladly you know," he said, half apologetically; "but by all accounts you are not a fool, eh, M. Poirot?"

He laughed breezily.

"Those who have thought so have been sadly mistaken," said Poirot placidly.

"Is that so? Well, so Nancy has carted you down here—got a bee in her bonnet about the secretary. There is nothing in that. Trefusis is as mild as milk—drinks milk, too, I believe. The fellow is a teetotaler. Rather waste of your time, isn't it?"

"If one has an opportunity to observe human nature, time is never wasted," said Poirot quietly.

"Human nature, eh?"

Victor Astwell stared at him; then he flung himself down in a chair.

"Anything I can do for you?"

"Yes, you can tell me what your quarrel with your brother was about that evening."

Victor Astwell shook his head.

"Nothing to do with the case," he said decisively.

"One can never be sure," said Poirot.

"It had nothing to do with Charles Leverson."

"Lady Astwell thinks that Charles had nothing to do with the murder."

"Oh! Nancy."

"Parsons assumes that it was M. Charles Leverson who came in that night, but he didn't see him. Remember—nobody saw him."

"You are wrong there," said Astwell, "*I* saw him."

"You saw him?"

"It's very simple. Reuben had been pitching into young Charles—not without good reason, I must say—later on he tried to bully me. I told him a few home truths and, just to annoy him, I made up my mind to back the boy. I meant to see him that night so as to tell him how the land lay. When I went up to my room I didn't go to bed; instead, I left the door ajar and sat on a chair smoking. My room is on the second floor, M. Poirot, and Charles's room is next to it."

"Pardon my interrupting you, M. Trefusis—he, too, sleeps on that floor?"

Astwell nodded.

"Yes, his room is just beyond mine."

"Nearer the stairs?"

"No; the other way."

A curious light came into Poirot's face, but the other didn't notice it, and went on:

"As I say, I waited up for Charles. I heard the front door slam, as I thought, about five minutes to twelve, but there was no sign of Charles for about ten minutes. When he did come up the stairs, I saw that it was no good tackling him that night."

He lifted his elbow significantly.

"I see," murmured Poirot discreetly.

"Poor devil couldn't walk straight," said Astwell. "He was looking pretty ghastly, too. I put it down to his condition at the time; of course, now I realize that he had come straight from committing the crime."

Poirot interposed a quick question.

"You heard nothing from the Tower room?"

Astwell shook his head.

"No; but you must remember that I was right at the other end of the building. The walls are thick, and I don't believe you would even hear a pistol shot fired from there."

Poirot nodded.

"I asked if he would like some help getting to bed," continued Astwell, "but he said he was all right and went into his room and banged the door. I undressed and went to bed and thought no more of it."

Poirot was staring thoughtfully at the carpet.

"You realize, M. Astwell," he said at last, "that your evidence is very important?"

"I suppose so, at least—what do you mean?"

"Your evidence that ten minutes elapsed between the slamming of the front door and Leverson's appearance upstairs. He himself says, so I understand, that he came into the house and went straight up to bed. But there is more than that. Lady Astwell's accusation of the secretary is fantastic, I admit, yet up to now it has not been proved impossible. But your evidence creates an *alibi*."

"How is that?"

"Lady Astwell says that she left her husband at a quarter to twelve. The only time he could have committed the crime was between a quarter to twelve and Charles Leverson's return. Now, if, as you say, you sat with your door open, he could not have come down from his room without your seeing him."

"That is so," agreed the other.

"There is no other staircase?"

"No; to get down to the Tower room he would have had to pass my door, and he didn't; I am quite sure of that. And anyway, M. Poirot, as I said just now, the man is as meek as a parson, I assure you."

"But yes, but yes," said Poirot soothingly, "I understand all that." He paused. "And you will not tell me the subject of your quarrel with Sir Reuben?"

The other's face turned a dark red.

"You'll get nothing out of me," he growled.

Poirot looked at the ceiling.

"I can always be discreet," he murmured, "where a lady is concerned."

Victor Astwell sprang to his feet.

"Damn you, how did you—what do you mean?"

"I was thinking," said Poirot, "of Miss Lily Margrave."

Victor Astwell stood undecided for a minute or two, then his colour subsided, and he sat down again.

"You are too clever for me, M. Poirot. Yes; it was Lily we quarrelled about. Reuben had his knife into her; he had ferretted out something or other about the girl—false references—something of that kind. I don't believe a word of it myself. And then he went further than he had any right to go; talked about her stealing down at night and getting out of the house to meet some fellow or other. My God! I gave it to him. I told him that better men than he had been killed for saying less. That shut him up. Reuben was inclined to be a bit afraid of me when I got going."

"I hardly wonder at it," murmured Poirot politely.

"I think a lot of Lily Margrave," said Victor in another tone. "A nice girl, through and through; I'd go bail for her anywhere."

Poirot did not answer, he was staring in front of him, seemingly lost in abstraction. He came out of his brown study with a jerk.

"I must, I think, promenade myself a little. There is an hotel here, yes?"

"Two," said Victor Astwell; "the Golf Hotel up by the links, and the Mitre down by the station, both pretty decent."

"I thank you," said Poirot. "Yes, certainly, I must promenade myself a little."

CHAPTER VI

THE Golf Hotel, as befits its name, stands on the Golf Links almost adjoining the Club House. It was to this hostelry that Poirot repaired first, in the course of that "promenade," which he had advertised himself as being about to take. The little man had his own way of doing things. Three minutes after he had entered the Golf Hotel, he was in private consultation with Miss Langdon, the Manageress.

"I regret to incommode you in any way, Mademoiselle," said Poirot; "but, you see, I am a detective."

Simplicity always appealed to him. In this case the method proved efficacious at once.

"A detective!" exclaimed Miss Langdon, looking at him doubtfully.

"Not from Scotland Yard," Poirot assured her. "In fact—you may have noticed it?—I am not an Englishman. No;

I make the private inquiries into the death of Sir Reuben Astwell."

"You don't say so!" Miss Langdon goggled at him expectantly.

"Precisely," said Poirot beaming. "Only to someone of discretion, like yourself, would I reveal the fact. I think, Mademoiselle, you may be able to aid me. Can you tell me of any gentleman staying here on the night of the murder who was absent from the Hotel that evening, and returned to it about twelve or half past?"

Miss Langdon's eyes opened wider than ever.

"You don't think——?" she breathed.

"That you had the murderer here? Ah, indeed that would be farcical! No; but I have reason to believe that a guest staying here promenaded himself in the direction of Mon Repos that night, and if so he may have seen something which, though conveying no meaning to him, might be very useful to me."

The Manageress nodded her head sapiently, with an air of one thoroughly well up in the annals of detective law.

"I understand perfectly. Now, let me see, who did we have staying here just then?"

She frowned, evidently running over the names in her mind, and helping her memory by occasionally checking them off on her finger-tips.

"Captain Swann, Mr. Elkins, Major Blunt, old Mr. Benson. No, really, sir, I don't believe anyone went out that evening."

"You would have noticed if they had done so, eh?"

"Oh yes, sir, it is not very usual you see. I mean, gentlemen go out to dinner and all that, but they don't go out after dinner, because—well, there is nowhere to go to, is there?"

The attractions of Abbot's Cross were Golf and nothing but Golf. It did not even boast a picture house.

"That is so," agreed Poirot. "Then as far as you remember, Mademoiselle, nobody from here was out that night?"

"Captain England and his wife were out to dinner."

Poirot shook his head.

"That is not the kind of thing I mean. I will try the other hotel, the Mitre, is it not?"

"Oh! the Mitre," said Miss Langdon; "of course, anyone might have gone out walking from there."

The disparagement of her tone, though vapid, was evident, and Poirot beat a tactful retreat. Ten minutes later he was repeating the scene, this time with Miss Cole, the brusque manageress of the Mitre, a less pretentious hotel with lower prices, situated close to the station.

"There was one gentleman out late that night; came in about half-past twelve, as far as I can remember. Quite a habit of his it was, to go out for a walk at that time of the evening. He had done it once or twice before. Let me see now, what was his name? Just for the moment I can't remember it."

She pulled a large ledger towards her, and began turning over the pages.

"Nineteenth, twentieth, twenty-first, twenty-second—Ah, here we are, Naylor—Captain Humphrey Naylor."

"He had stayed here before; you know him well?"

"Once before," said Miss Cole, "about a fortnight earlier. He went out then in the evening, I remember."

"He came to play the golf, eh?"

"I suppose so," said Miss Cole, "that's what most of the gentlemen come for."

"Very true," said Poirot. "Well, Mademoiselle, I thank you infinitely, and I wish you good-day."

He went back to Mon Repos with a very thoughtful face. Once or twice he drew something from his pocket and looked at it.

"It must be done," he murmured to himself, "and soon, as soon as I can make the opportunity."

His first proceeding on re-entering the house was to ask Parsons where Miss Margrave might be found. He was told that she was in the small study dealing with Lady Astwell's correspondence, and the information seemed to afford Poirot satisfaction. He found the little study without difficulty. Lily Margrave was seated at a desk by the window, writing. But for her the room was empty. Poirot carefully shut the door behind him, and came towards the girl.

"I may have a little minute of your time, Mademoiselle, you will be so kind?"

"Certainly."

Lily Margrave put the papers aside and turned towards him.

"What can I do for you?"

"On the evening of the tragedy, Mademoiselle, I understand that when Lady Astwell went to her husband you went straight up to bed. Is that so?"

Lily Margrave nodded.

"You did not come down again by any chance?"

The girl shook her head.

"I think you said, Mademoiselle, that you had not at any time that evening been in the Tower room."

"I don't remember saying so, but as a matter of fact that is quite true. I was not in the Tower room that evening."

Poirot raised his eyebrows.

"Curious," he murmured.

"What do you mean?"

"Very curious," murmured Hercule Poirot again. "How do you account then for this?"

He drew from his pocket a little scrap of stained green chiffon, and held it up for the girl's inspection.

Her expression did not change; but he felt, rather than heard, the sharp intake of breath.

"I don't understand, M. Poirot."

"You wore, I understand, a green chiffon dress that evening, Mademoiselle. This," he tapped the scrap in his fingers, "was torn from it."

"And you found it in the Tower room?" asked the girl sharply. "Whereabouts?"

Hercule Poirot looked at the ceiling.

"For the moment shall we just say—in the Tower room?"

For the first time a look of fear sprang into the girl's eyes. She began to speak, then checked herself. Poirot watched her small white hands clenching themselves on the edge of the desk.

"I wonder if I did go into the Tower

room that evening?" she mused, "before dinner, I mean. I don't think so—I am almost sure I didn't. If that scrap has been in the Tower room all this time, it seems to me a very extraordinary thing the police did not find it earlier."

"The police," said the little man, "do not think of the things that Hercule Poirot thinks of." And he smiled to himself.

"I may have run in there for a minute just before dinner," mused Lily Margrave, "or it may have been the night before. I wore the same dress then. Yes; I am almost sure it was the night before."

"I think not," said Poirot evenly.

"Why?"

He only shook his head slowly from side to side.

"What do you mean?" whispered the girl.

She was leaning forward, staring at him, all the colour ebbing out of her face.

"You do not notice, Mademoiselle, that this fragment is stained? There is no doubt about it, that stain is human blood."

"You mean——"

"I mean, Mademoiselle, that you were in the Tower room *after* the crime was committed, not before. I think you will do well to tell me the whole truth, lest worse should befall you."

He stood up now, a stern little figure of a man, his forefinger pointing accusingly at the girl.

"How did you find out?" gasped Lily.

"No matter, Mademoiselle; I tell you Hercule Poirot *knows*. I know all about Captain Humphrey Naylor, and that you went down to meet him that night."

Lily suddenly put her head down on her arms and burst into tears. Immediately, Poirot relinquished his accusing attitude. He became almost paternal.

"There, there, my little one," he said, patting the girl on the shoulder. "Do not distress yourself. Impossible to deceive Hercule Poirot; once realize that, and all your troubles will be at an end. And now you will tell me the whole story, will you not? You will tell old Papa Poirot?"

"It is not what you think, it isn't indeed·

Humphrey—my brother—never touched a hair of his head."

"Your brother, eh?" said Poirot. "So that is how the land lies. Well, if you wish to save him from suspicion, you must tell me the whole story now—without reservations, you understand?"

Lily sat up again, pushing back the hair from her forehead. After a minute or two, she began to speak in a low, clear voice.

"I will tell you the truth, M. Poirot. I can see now that it would be absurd to do anything else. My real name is Lily Naylor, and Humphrey is my only brother. Some years ago, when he was out in Africa, he discovered a gold mine, or rather I should say discovered the presence of gold. I can't tell you this part of it properly, because I don't understand the technical details, but what it amounted to was this: The thing seemed likely to be a very big undertaking, and Humphrey came home with letters to Sir Reuben Astwell in the hopes of getting him interested in the matter. I don't understand the rights of it even now; but I gather that Sir Reuben sent out an expert to report, and that he subsequently told my brother that the expert's report was unfavourable and that he, Humphrey, had made a great mistake. My brother went back to Africa on an expedition into the interior, and was lost sight of. It was assumed that he and the expedition had perished. It was soon after that, that a company was formed to exploit the Mpala Gold Fields. When my brother got back to England, he at once jumped to the conclusion that these gold fields were identical with those he had discovered. Sir Reuben Astwell had apparently nothing to do with this company, and they had seemingly discovered the place on their own. But my brother was not satisfied; he was convinced that Sir Reuben had deliberately swindled him. He became more and more violent and unhappy about the matter. We two are alone in the world, M. Poirot, and as it was necessary then for me to go out and earn my own living, I conceived the idea of taking a post in this household and trying to find out if any connection existed between Sir Reuben and the Mpala Gold Fields. For obvious reasons I concealed my real name, and I'll admit, frankly, that I used a forged reference. There were many applicants for the post, most of them with better qualifications than mine, so—well, M. Poirot, I wrote a beautiful letter from the Duchess of Perthshire, who I knew had just gone to America. I thought a Duchess would have a great effect upon Lady Astwell, and I was quite right—she engaged me on the spot. Since then I have been that hateful thing, a spy, and until lately with no success. Sir Reuben is not a man to give away his business secrets; but when Victor Astwell came back from Africa he was less guarded in his talk, and I began to believe that after all Humphrey had not been mistaken. My brother came down here about a fortnight before the murder, and I crept out of the house to meet him secretly at night. I told him the things Victor Astwell had said, and he became very excited, and assured me I was on the right track.

"But after that things began to go wrong; someone must have seen me stealing out of the house and have reported the matter to Sir Reuben. He became suspicious and hunted up my references, and soon discovered the fact that they were forged. The crisis came on the day of the murder. I think he thought I was after his wife's jewels. Whatever his suspicions were, he had no intention of allowing me to remain any longer at Mon Repos, though he agreed not to prosecute me on account of the references. Lady Astwell took my part throughout, and stood up valiantly to Sir Reuben."

She paused. Poirot's face was very grave.

"And now, Mademoiselle," he said, "we come to the night of the murder."

Lily swallowed hard, and nodded her head.

"To begin with, M. Poirot, I must tell you that my brother had come down again, and that I had arranged to steal out and meet him once more. I went up to my room as I have said, but I did not go to bed; instead, I waited till I thought everyone was asleep and then stole downstairs again, and out by the side-door. I met Humphrey and acquainted him in a few hurried words with what had occurred. I told him that I believed the papers he wanted were in Sir Reuben's safe in the Tower room, and we agreed as a last desperate adventure to try and get hold of them that night. I was to go in first and see that the way was clear. I heard the church clock strike twelve as I went in by the side-door. I was half-way up the stairs leading to the Tower room when I heard a thud of something falling, and a voice cried out: 'My God!' A minute or two afterwards the door of the Tower room opened, and Charles Leverson came out. I could see his face quite clearly in the moonlight, but I was crouching some way below him on the stairs where it was dark, and he did not see me. He stood there a moment swaying on his feet and looking ghastly. He seemed to be listening, then with an effort he seemed to pull himself together, and opening the door into the

Tower room called out something about there being no harm done. His voice was quite jaunty and debonair, but his face gave the lie to it. He waited a minute more, and then slowly went on upstairs and out of sight.

"When he had gone I waited a minute or two and then crept to the Tower room door. I had a feeling that something tragic had happened. The main light was out, but the desk lamp was on, and by its light I saw Sir Reuben lying in a huddled mass on the floor by the desk. I don't know how I managed it, but I nerved myself at last to go over and kneel down by him. I saw at once that he was dead, struck down from behind, and also that he couldn't have been dead long; I touched his hand and it was still quite warm. It was horrible, M. Poirot, horrible."

She shuddered again at the remembrance.

"And then?" said Poirot looking at her keenly.

Lily Margrave nodded.

"Yes, M. Poirot, I know what you are thinking. Why didn't I give the alarm and

rouse the house? I should have done, I
know; but it came over me in a flash as I
knelt there, that my quarrel with Sir Reuben,
my stealing out to meet Humphrey, and
the fact that I was being sent away on
the morrow made a fatal sequence. They
would say that I let Humphrey in, and that
Humphrey had killed Sir Reuben out of
revenge. If I said that I had seen Charles
Leverson leaving the room no one would
believe me. It was terrible, M. Poirot. I
knelt there, and thought and thought, and
the more I thought the more my nerve
failed me. Presently I noticed Sir Reuben's
keys which had dropped from his pocket
as he fell. Among them was the key of the
safe; the combination word I already knew,
since Lady Astwell had mentioned it once
in my hearing. I went over to that safe, M.
Poirot; I unlocked it and rummaged through
the papers. In the end I found what I
was looking for. Humphrey had been
perfectly right, Sir Reuben was behind the
Mpala Gold Fields, and he had deliberately
swindled Humphrey. That made it all the
worse; it gave a perfectly definite motive for

Humphrey having committed the crime. I put the papers back in the safe, left the key in the door of it, and went straight upstairs to my room. In the morning I pretended to be surprised and horror-stricken like everyone else when the house-maid discovered the body."

She stopped and looked piteously across at Poirot.

"You do believe me, M. Poirot? Oh, do say you believe me!"

"I believe you, Mademoiselle," said Poirot. "You have explained many things that puzzled me. Your absolute certainty, for one thing, that Charles Leverson had committed the crime, and at the same time your persistent efforts to keep me from coming down here."

Lily nodded.

"I was afraid of you," she admitted frankly. "Lady Astwell could not know, as I did, that Charles was guilty, and I couldn't say anything. I hoped against hope that you would refuse to take the case."

'But for that obvious anxiety on your

part, I might have done so," said Poirot drily.

Lily looked at him swiftly; her lips trembled a little.

"And now, M. Poirot, what—what are you going to do?"

"As far as you are concerned, Mademoiselle, nothing. I believe your story, and I accept it. The next step is to go to London and see Inspector Miller."

"And then?" asked Lily.

"And then," said Poirot, "we shall see."

Outside the door of the study, he looked once more at the little square of stained green chiffon in his hand.

"Amazing," he murmured to himself complacently, "the ingenuity of Hercule Poirot."

CHAPTER VII

DETECTIVE-INSPECTOR MILLER was not particularly fond of M. Hercule Poirot. He did not belong to that small band of Inspectors at the Yard who welcomed the little Belgian's co-operation. He was wont to say that Hercule Poirot was much over-rated. In this case he felt pretty sure of himself, and greeted Poirot with high good humour in consequence.

"Acting for Lady Astwell, are you? Well, you have taken up a mare's nest in that case."

"There is, then, no possible doubt about the matter?"

Miller winked.

"Never was a clearer case, short of catching a murderer absolutely red-handed."

"Mr. Leverson has made a statement, I understand?"

"He had better have kept his mouth

shut," said the detective. "He repeats over and over again that he went straight up to his room and never went near his uncle. That's a fool story on the face of it."

"It is certainly against the weight of evidence," murmured Poirot. "How does he strike you, this young Mr. Leverson?"

"Darned young fool."

"A weak character, eh?"

The Inspector nodded.

"One would hardly think a young man of that type would have the—how do you say it?—the guts to commit such a crime."

"On the face of it, no," agreed the Inspector. "But bless you, I have come across the same thing many times. Get a weak, dissipated young man into a corner, fill him up with a drop too much to drink, and for a limited amount of time you can turn him into a fire eater. A weak man in a corner is more dangerous than a strong man."

"That is true, yes, that is true what you say."

Miller unbent a little further.

"Of course, it is all right for you, M. Poirot," he said. "You get your fees just the same, and naturally you have to make a pretence of examining the evidence to satisfy her ladyship. I can understand all that."

"You understand such interesting things," murmured Poirot, and took his leave.

His next call was upon the solicitor representing Charles Leverson. Mr. Mayhew was a thin, dry, cautious gentleman. He received Poirot with reserve. Poirot, however, had his own ways of inducing confidence. In ten minutes time the two were talking together amicably.

"You will understand," said Poirot, "I am acting in this case solely on behalf of Mr. Leverson. That is Lady Astwell's wish. She is convinced that he is not guilty."

"Yes, yes, quite so," said Mr. Mayhew without enthusiasm.

Poirot's eyes twinkled.

"You do not perhaps attach much

importance to the opinions of Lady Ast-well?" he suggested.

"She might be just as sure of his guilt to-morrow," said the lawyer drily.

"Her intuitions are not evidence, cer-tainly," agreed Poirot; "and on the face of it the case looks very black against this poor young man."

"It is a pity he said what he did to the police," said the lawyer. "It will be no good his sticking to that story."

"Has he stuck to it to you?" inquired Poirot.

Mayhew nodded.

"It never varies an iota. He repeats it like a parrot."

"And that is what destroys your faith in him," mused the other. "Ah! don't deny it," he added quickly, holding up an arresting hand, "I see it only too plainly. In your heart you believe him guilty. But listen now to me, to me, Hercule Poirot. I present to you a case. This young man comes home, he has drunk the cocktail, the cocktail, and again the cocktail, also without doubt the English whisky-and-soda many times! He is full of—what you call it?—the courage Dutch, and in that mood he lets himself into the house with his latch-key, and he goes with unsteady steps up to the Tower room. He looks in at the door and sees in the dim light his uncle, apparently bending over the desk. Mr. Leverson is full, as we have said, of the courage Dutch. He lets himself go, he tells his uncle just what he thinks of him. He defies him, he insults him, and the more his uncle does not answer back, the more he is encouraged to go on, to repeat himself, to say the same thing over and over again, and each time more loudly. But at last the continued silence of his uncle awakens an apprehension. He goes nearer to him, he lays his hand on his uncle's shoulder, and his uncle's figure crumples under his touch and sinks in a heap to the ground. He is sobered then, Mr. Leverson; the chair falls with a crash, and he bends over Sir Reuben. He realizes what has happened, he looks at his hand covered with something warm and red. He is in a panic then; he would give anything on earth to recall the cry which has just sprung from his lips, echoing through the house. Mechanically he picks up the chair; then he hastens out through the door and listens. He fancies he hears a sound, and immediately, automatically, he pretends to be speaking to his uncle through the open door. The sound is not repeated; he is convinced he has been mistaken in thinking he heard one. Now all is silence; he creeps up to his room, and at once it occurs to him how much better it will be if he pretends never to have been near his uncle that night. So he tells his story. Parsons at that time, remember, has said nothing of what he heard. When he does do so, it is too late for Mr. Leverson to change. He is stupid, and he is obstinate—he sticks to his story. Tell me, Monsieur, is that not possible?"

"Yes," said the lawyer, "I suppose in the way you put it, that it is possible."

Poirot rose to his feet.

"You have the privilege of seeing Mr. Leverson," he said. "Put to him the story I have told you, and ask him if it is not true."

Outside the lawyer's office, Poirot hailed a taxi.

"348 Harley Street," he murmured to the driver.

CHAPTER VIII

POIROT's departure for London had taken
Lady Astwell by surprise, for the little
man had not made any mention of what
he proposed doing. On his return, after
an absence of twenty-four hours, he was
informed by Parsons that Lady Astwell
would like to see him as soon as possible.
Poirot found the lady in her own boudoir;
she was lying down on the divan, her
head propped up by cushions, and she
looked startlingly ill and haggard, far
more so than she had done on the day
Poirot arrived.

"So you have come back, M. Poirot?"

"I have returned, milady."

"You went to London?"

Poirot nodded.

"You didn't tell me you were going,"
said Lady Astwell sharply.

"A thousand apologies, milady; I am
in error, I should have done so. *La
prochaine fois*——"

"You will do exactly the same," interrupted Lady Astwell with a shrewd touch of humour. "Do things first and tell people afterwards, that is your motto right enough."

"Perhaps it has also been milady's motto?" his eyes twinkled.

"Now and then perhaps," admitted the other. "What did you go up to London for, M. Poirot. You can tell me now, I suppose?"

"I had an interview with the good Inspector Miller, and also with the excellent Mr. Mayhew."

Lady Astwell's eyes searched his face. "And you think now——?" she said slowly.

Poirot's eyes were fixed on her steadily.

"That there is a possibility of Charles Leverson's innocence," he said gravely.

"Ah!" Lady Astwell half sprang up, sending two cushions rolling to the ground. "I was right, then, I was right."

"I said a possibility, madame, that is all."

Something in his tone seemed to strike her. She raised herself on one elbow and regarded him piercingly.

"Can I do anything?" she asked.

"Yes," he nodded his head, "you can tell me, Lady Astwell, why you suspect Owen Trefusis."

"I have told you, I *know*—that's all."

"Unfortunately that is not enough," said Poirot drily. "Cast your mind back to the fatal evening, milady. Remember each detail, each tiny happening; what did you notice or observe about the secretary? I, Hercule Poirot, tell you there must have been something."

Lady Astwell shook her head.

"I hardly noticed him at all that evening," she said; "and I certainly was not thinking of him."

"Your mind was taken up by something else?"

"Yes."

"With your husband's animus against Miss Lily Margrave?"

"That's right," said Lady Astwell, nodding her head; "you seem to know all about it, M. Poirot."

"Me, I know everything," declared the little man grandiloquently.

"I am fond of Lily, M. Poirot; you have seen that for yourself. Reuben began kicking up a rumpus about some reference or other of hers. Mind you, I don't say she hadn't cheated about it, she had; but, bless you, I have done many worse things than that in the old days. You have got to be up to all sorts of tricks to get round theatrical managers. There is nothing I wouldn't have written, or said, or done, in my time. Lily wanted this job, and she put in a lot of slick work that was not quite —well, quite the thing, you know. Men are so stupid about that sort of thing. Lily really might have been a bank clerk absconding with millions for the fuss he made about it. I was terribly worried all the evening, because although I could usually get round Reuben in the end, he was terribly pig-headed at times, poor darling. So, of course, I hadn't time to go noticing secretaries—not that one does notice Mr. Trefusis much, anyway. He is just there and that's all there is to it."

"I have noticed that fact about M. Trefusis," said Poirot. "His is not a personality that stands forth, that shines, that hits you cr-r-rack."

"No," said Lady Astwell, "he is not like Victor."

"Mr. Victor Astwell is, I should say, explosive."

"That is a splendid word for him," said Lady Astwell. "He explodes all over the house, like one of those thingimy-jig firework things."

"A somewhat quick temper, I should imagine?" suggested Poirot.

"Oh, he's a perfect devil when roused," said Lady Astwell; "but, bless you, *I'm* not afraid of him. All bark and no bite to Victor."

Poirot looked at the ceiling.

"And you can tell me nothing about the secretary that evening?" he murmured gently.

"I tell you, M. Poirot, I *know*. It's intuition. A woman's intuition——"

"Will not hang a man," said Poirot, "and what is more to the point, it will not save a man from being hanged. Lady Astwell, if you sincerely believe that Mr. Leverson is innocent, and that your suspicions of the secretary are well founded, will you consent to a little experiment?"

"What kind of an experiment?" demanded Lady Astwell suspiciously.

"Will you permit yourself to be put into a condition of hypnosis?"

"Whatever for?"

Poirot leaned forward.

"If I were to tell you, madame, that your intuition is based on certain facts recorded subconsciously, you would probably be sceptical. I will only say, then, that this experiment I propose may be of great importance to that unfortunate young man, Charles Leverson. You will not refuse?"

"Who is going to put me into a trance?" demanded Lady Astwell suspiciously. "You?"

"A friend of mine, Lady Astwell, arrives, if I mistake not, at this very minute. I hear the wheels of the car outside."

"Who is he?"

"A Dr. Cazalet of Harley Street."

"Is he—all right?" asked Lady Astwell apprehensively.

"He is not a quack, madame, if that is what you mean. You can trust yourself in his hands quite safely."

"Well," said Lady Astwell with a sigh, "I think it *is* all bunkum, but you can try if you like. Nobody is going to say that I stood in your way."

"A thousand thanks, milady."

Poirot hurried from the room. In a few minutes he returned ushering in a cheerful, round-faced little man, with spectacles, who was very upsetting to Lady Astwell's conception of what an hypnotist should look like.

Poirot then introduced them.

"Well," said Lady Astwell good humouredly, "how do we start this tom-foolery?"

"Quite simple, Lady Astwell, quite simple," said the little doctor. "Just lean back, so—that's right, that's right. No need to be uneasy."

"I am not in the least uneasy," said Lady Astwell; "I should like to see anyone hypnotizing me against my will."

Dr. Cazalet smiled broadly.

"Yes, but if you consent, it won't be against your will, will it?" he said cheerfully. "That's right. Turn off that other light will you, M. Poirot? Just let yourself go to sleep, Lady Astwell."

He shifted his position a little.

"It's getting late. You are sleepy—very sleepy. Your eyelids are heavy, they are closing—closing—closing. Soon you will be asleep. . . ."

His voice droned on, low, soothing and monotonous. Presently he leaned forward and gently lifted Lady Astwell's right eyelid. Then he turned to Poirot, nodding in a satisfied manner.

"That's all right," he said in a low voice. "Shall I go ahead?"

"If you please."

The doctor spoke out sharply and authoritatively:

"You are asleep, Lady Astwell, but you hear me, and you can answer my questions."

Without stirring or raising an eyelid, the motionless figure on the sofa replied in a low monotonous voice:

"I hear you; I can answer your questions."

"Lady Astwell, I want you to go back to the evening on which your husband was murdered. You remember that evening?"

"Yes."

"You are at the dinner table. Describe to me what you saw and felt."

The prone figure stirred a little restlessly.

"I am in great distress; I am worried about Lily."

"We know that, tell us what you saw."

"Victor is eating all the salted almonds, he is greedy. To-morrow I shall tell Parsons not to put the dish that side of the table."

"Go on, Lady Astwell."

"Reuben is in a bad humour to-night. I don't think it is altogether about Lily, it is something to do with business; Victor looks at him in a queer way."

"Tell us about Mr. Trefusis, Lady Astwell."

"His left shirt cuff is frayed. He puts a lot of grease on his hair. I wish men didn't, it ruins the covers in the drawing-room."

Cazalet looked at Poirot, the other made a motion with his head.

"It is after dinner, Lady Astwell; you are having coffee. Describe the scene to me."

"The coffee is good to-night. It varies; cook is very unreliable over her coffee. Lily keeps looking out of the window, I don't know why. Now Reuben comes into the room; he is in one of his worst moods to-night, and bursts out with a perfect flood of abuse to poor Mr. Trefusis. Mr. Trefusis has got his hand round the paper-knife, the big one with the sharp blade like a knife. How hard he is grasping it, his knuckles are quite white. Look! he has dug it so hard in the table, that the point snaps. He holds it just as you would hold a dagger you were going to stick into some-one. There, they have gone out together now. Lily has got her green evening dress on; she looks so pretty in green, just like a lily. I must have the covers cleaned next week. . . .

"Just a minute, Lady Astwell."

The doctor leaned across to Poirot.

"We have got it, I think," he murmured; "that action with the paper-knife, that's what convinced her that the secretary did the thing."

"Let us go on to the Tower room now."

The doctor nodded, and began once more to question Lady Astwell in his high decisive voice.

"It is later in the evening; you are in the Tower room with your husband. You and he have had a terrible scene together, have you not?"

Again the figure stirred uneasily.

"Yes—terrible—terrible. We said dreadful things—both of us."

"Never mind that now. You can see the room clearly, the curtains were drawn, the lights were on."

"Not the middle light, only the desk light."

"You are leaving your husband now, you are saying good-night to him."

"No; I was too angry."

"It is the last time you will see him, very soon he will be murdered. Do you know who murdered him, Lady Astwell."

"Yes; Mr. Trefusis."

"Why do you say that?"

"Because of the bulge—the bulge in the curtain."

"There was a bulge in the curtain?"

"Yes."

"You saw it?"

"Yes; I almost touched it."

"Was it a man concealed there? Mr. Trefusis?"

"Yes."

"How do you know?"

For the first time the monotonous answering voice hesitated, and lost confidence.

"I—I—because of the paper-knife."

Poirot and the doctor again interchanged swift glances.

"I don't understand you, Lady Astwell. There was a bulge in the curtain, you say? Someone concealed there? You didn't see that person?"

"No."

"You thought it was Mr. Trefusis because of the way he held the paper-knife earlier?"

"Yes."

"But Mr. Trefusis had gone upstairs, had he not?

"Yes—yes, that's right, he had gone upstairs."

"So he couldn't have been behind the curtain in the window."

"No—no, of course not, he wasn't there."

"He had said good-night to your husband some time before, hadn't he?"

"Yes."

"And you didn't see him again?"

"No."

She was stirring now, throwing herself about, moaning faintly.

"She is coming out," said the doctor. "Well, I think we have got all we can, eh?"

Poirot nodded. The doctor leaned over Lady Astwell.

"You are waking," he murmured softly. "You are waking now, in another minute you will open your eyes."

The two men waited, and presently Lady Astwell suddenly sat upright and stared at them both.

"Have I been having a nap?"

"That's it, Lady Astwell, just a little sleep," said the doctor.

She looked at him.

"Some of your *hocus pocus*, eh?"

"You don't feel any the worse I hope?" he asked.

Lady Astwell yawned.

"I feel rather tired and done up."

The doctor rose.

"I will ask them to send you up some coffee," he said, "and we will leave you for the present."

"Did I—say anything?" Lady Astwell called after them as they reached the door.

Poirot smiled back at her.

"Nothing of great importance, madame; you informed us that the drawing-room covers needed cleaning.

"So they do," said Lady Astwell; "you needn't have put me into a trance to get me to tell you that." She laughed good humouredly. "Anything more?"

"Do you remember M. Trefusis picking up a paper-knife in the drawing-room that night?" asked Poirot.

"I don't know, I'm sure," said Lady Astwell; "he may have done so."

"Does a bulge in the curtain convey anything to you?"

Lady Astwell frowned.

"I seem to remember," she said slowly; "no—it's gone, and yet——"

"Do not distress yourself Lady Astwell," said Poirot quickly, "it is of no importance —of no importance whatever."

The doctor went with Poirot to the latter's room.

"Well," said Cazalet, "I think this explains things pretty clearly. No doubt when Sir Reuben was dressing down the secretary the latter grabbed tight hold of a paper-knife, and had to exercise a good deal of self-control to prevent himself answering back. Lady Astwell's conscious mind was wholly taken up with the problem of Lily Margrave, but her subconscious mind noticed and misconstrued the action. It implanted in her the firm conviction that Trefusis murdered Sir Reuben. Now we come to the bulge in the curtain. That is interesting. I take it from what you have told me of the Tower room, that the desk was right in the window. There are curtains across that window, of course?"

"Yes, *mon ami*, black velvet curtains."

"And there is room in the embrasure of the window for anyone to remain concealed behind them?"

"There would be just room, I think."

"Then there seems at least a possibility," said the doctor slowly, "that someone was concealed in the room, but if so it could not be the secretary, since they both saw him leave the room. It could not be Victor Astwell, for Trefusis met him going out, and it could not be Lily Margrave. Whoever it was must have been concealed there before Sir Reuben entered the room that evening. You have told me pretty well how the land lies. Now, what about Captain Naylor—could it have been he who was concealed there?"

"It is always possible," admitted Poirot. "He certainly dined at the hotel, but how soon he went out afterwards is difficult to fix exactly. He returned about half-past twelve."

"Then it might have been him," said the doctor, "and if so, he committed the crime. He had the motive, and there was a weapon near at hand. You don't seem satisfied with the idea though?"

"Me, I have other ideas," confessed Poirot. "Tell me now, M. le Docteur, supposing for one minute that Lady Astwell herself had committed this crime, would she necessarily betray the fact in the hypnotic state?"

The doctor whistled.

"So that's what you are getting at. Lady Astwell is the criminal, eh? Of course—it is possible. I never thought of it till this minute. She was the last to be with him, and no one saw him alive afterwards. As to your question, I should be inclined to say 'No.' Lady Astwell would go into the hypnotic state with a strong mental reservation to say nothing of her own part in the crime. She would answer my questions truthfully, but she would be dumb on that one point. Yet I should hardly have expected her to be so insistent on Mr. Trefusis's guilt. But I have not said that I believe Lady Astwill to be the criminal. It is a supposition, that is all."

"I comprehend," said Poirot.

"It is an interesting case," said the doctor after a minute or two. Granting Charles Leverson is innocent, there are so many possibilities: Humphrey Naylor, Lady Astwell, and even Lily Margrave."

"There is another you have not mentioned," said Poirot quietly. "Victor Astwell. According to his own story, he sat in his room with the door open waiting for Charles Leverson's return, but we have only his own word for it, you comprehend?"

"He is the bad-tempered fellow, isn't he?" asked the doctor. "The one you told me about?"

"That is so," agreed Poirot.

The doctor rose to his feet.

"Well, I must be getting back to town, ought to do it in three-quarters of an hour at this time of night. You will let me know how things shape, won't you?"

After the doctor had left, Poirot pressed the bell for George.

"A cup of *tisane*, George. My nerves are much disturbed."

"Certainly, sir," said George; "I will prepare it immediately."

Ten minutes later he brought a steaming cup to his master. Poirot inhaled the noxious fumes with pleasure. As he sipped it, he soliloquized aloud.

"The chase is different all over the world. To catch the fox you ride hard with the dogs, you shout, you run—it is a matter of speed. I have not shot the stag myself, but I understand that to do so you crawl for many long, long hours upon your stomach. My friend Hastings has recounted the affair to me. Our method here, my good George, must be neither of these. Let us reflect instead upon the household cat. For many long, weary hours, he watches the mouse-hole, he makes no movement, he betrays no energy, but he—does not go away."

He sighed, and put the empty cup down on its saucer.

"I told you to pack for a few days. To-morrow, my good George, you will go to London and bring down what is necessary for a fortnight."

"Very good, sir," said George. As usual he displayed no emotion.

CHAPTER IX

THE apparently permanent presence of Hercule Poirot at Mon Repos was disquieting to many people. Victor Astwell remonstrated with his sister-in-law about it.

"It's all very well, Nancy, you don't know what fellows of that kind are like. He has found jolly comfortable quarters here, and he is evidently going to settle down comfortably for about a month, charging you two guineas a day all the while, I suppose."

Lady Astwell's reply was to the effect that she could manage her own affairs without outside interference.

Lily Margrave tried earnestly to conceal her perturbation. At the time, she had felt sure that Poirot believed her story. Now she was not so certain.

Poirot did not play an entirely quiescent game. On the fifth day of his sojourn he brought down a small thumbograph album to dinner. As a method of getting the thumb prints of the household it seemed a rather clumsy device, yet not perhaps so clumsy as it seemed, since no one could afford to refuse their thumb-prints. Only after the little man had retired to bed, did Victor Astwell state his views.

"You see what it means, Nancy, he is out after one of us."

"Don't be absurd, Victor."

"Well, what other meaning could that blinking little book of his have?"

"M. Poirot knows what he is doing," said Lady Astwell complacently.

She looked with some meaning at Owen Trefusis. On another occasion Poirot introduced the game of tracing foot-prints on a sheet of paper. The following morning, going with his soft, cat-like tread into the library, the detective startled Owen Trefusis, who leapt from his chair as though he had been shot.

"You must really excuse me, M. Poirot," he said primly, "but you have got us on the jump."

"Indeed, how is that?" demanded the little man innocently.

"I will admit," said the secretary, "that I thought the case against Charles Leverson utterly overwhelming; you, apparently, do not find it so."

Poirot was standing looking out of the window. He turned suddenly to the other.

"I will tell you something, Mr. Trefusis —in confidence."

"Yes?"

Poirot seemed in no hurry to begin. He waited a minute, hesitating. When he did speak, his opening words were coincident with the opening and shutting of the front door. For a man saying something in confidence, he spoke rather loud, his voice drowning the sound of a footstep in the hall outside.

"I will tell you this in confidence, Mr. Trefusis: there is new evidence. It goes to prove that when Charles Leverson entered the Tower room that night, Sir Reuben was already dead."

The secretary stared at him in amazement.

"But what evidence? Why have we not heard of it?"

"You *will* hear," said the little man mysteriously. "In the meantime, you and I alone know the secret."

He skipped nimbly out of the room and almost collided with Victor Astwell in the hall outside.

"You have just come in, eh, monsieur?"

Astwell nodded.

"Beastly day outside," he said, breathing hard; "cold and blowy."

"Ah!" said Poirot, "I shall not promenade myself to-day; me, I am like a cat, I sit by the fire and keep myself warm."

"*Ça marche*, George," he said that evening to the faithful valet, rubbing his hands as he spoke, "they are on the tenterhooks—the jump! It is hard, George, to play the game of the cat, the waiting game; but it answers, yes, it answers wonderfully. To-morrow we make a little further effect."

On the following day Trefusis was obliged to go up to town. He went up by the same train as Victor Astwell. No sooner had they left the house than Poirot was galvanized into a fever of activity.

"Come, George, let us hurry to work. If the housemaid should approach these rooms, you must delay her, speak to her sweet nothings, George, keep her in the corridor."

He went first to the secretary's room and began a thorough search. Not a drawer or a shelf was left uninspected. Then he replaced everything hurriedly, and declared his quest finished. George, on guard in the doorway, gave a deferential cough.

"If you will excuse me, sir?"

"Yes, my good George?"

"The shoes, sir. The two pairs of brown shoes were on the second shelf, and the patent leather ones were on the shelf underneath. In replacing them you have reversed the order."

"Marvellous!" cried Poirot holding up his hands. "But let us not distress ourselves over that. It is of no importance, I assure you, George; never will M. Trefusis notice such a trifling matter."

"As you think, sir," said George.

"It is your business to notice such things," said Poirot encouragingly, as he clapped the other on the shoulder. "It reflects credit upon you, great credit."

The valet did not reply, and when, later in the day, the proceeding was repeated in the room of Victor Astwell, he made no comment on the fact that Mr. Astwell's underclothing was not returned to its drawers strictly according to plan. Yet in the second case at least, events proved the valet to be right and Poirot wrong. Victor Astwell came storming into the drawing-room that evening.

"Now look here, you damned little Belgian jackanapes, what do you mean by searching my room? What the devil do you think you are going to find there? I won't have it, do you hear? That's what comes of having a nasty, ferreting little spy in the house."

Poirot's hands spread themselves out eloquently, as his words tumbled one over the other. He demanded a hundred apologies, a thousand, a million. He had been maladroit, officious, he was confused. He had taken an unwarranted liberty. In the end the infuriated gentleman was forced to subside, still growling inarticulately to himself.

And again that evening, sipping his *tisane*, Poirot murmured to George:

"It marches, my good George, yes—it marches."

CHAPTER X

"FRIDAY," observed Hercule Poirot thoughtfully, "is my lucky day."

"Indeed, sir."

"You are not superstitious perhaps, my good George?"

"I prefer not to sit down thirteen at table, sir, and I am averse to passing under ladders. I have no superstitions about a Friday, sir."

"That is well," said Poirot, "for see you, to-day we make our Waterloo."

"Really, sir."

"You have such enthusiasm, my good George, you do not even ask what I propose to do."

"And what is that, sir?"

Poirot leaned forward, shaking an emphatic forefinger.

"To-day, George, I make a final thorough search of the Tower room."

True enough, after breakfast, Poirot,

with the permission of Lady Astwell,
repaired to the scene of the crime. There,
at various times of the morning, members
of the household saw him crawling about
on all fours, examining minutely the black
velvet curtains, and standing on high chairs
to examine the picture frames on the
wall. Lady Astwell for the first time
displayed uneasiness.

"I have got to admit it," she said.
"He is getting on my nerves at last. He
has got something up his sleeve, and I
don't know what it is; and the way he is
crawling about on the floor up there like
a dog, makes me downright shivery. What
is he looking for, I'd like to know? Lily,
my dear, I wish you would go up and see
what he is up to now. No, on the whole,
I'd rather you stayed with me."

"Shall I go, Lady Astwell?" asked the
secretary, rising from the desk by the
window.

"If you would, Mr. Trefusis."

Owen Trefusis left the room and mounted
the stairs to the Tower room. At first
glance, he thought the room was empty;

there was certainly no sign of Hercule Poirot there. He was just turning to go down again when a sound caught his ears. He then saw the little man half-way down the spiral staircase that led to the bedroom above. He was on his hands and knees, in his left hand was a little pocket-lens, and through this he was examining minutely something on the woodwork beside the stair carpet. As the secretary watched him he uttered a sudden grunt, and slipped the lens in his pocket. He then rose to his feet, holding something between his finger and thumb. At that moment he became aware of the secretary's presence.

"Ah, ah! Mr. Trefusis, I didn't hear you enter."

He was in that moment a different man. Triumph and exultation beamed all over his face. Trefusis stared at him in surprise.

"What is the matter, M. Poirot? You look very pleased with yourself."

The little man puffed out his chest importantly.

"Yes, indeed. See you, I have at last

found that which I have been looking for from the beginning. I have here, between my finger and thumb, the one thing necessary to convict the criminal."

"Then," the secretary raised his eyebrows, "it was not Charles Leverson?"

"It was not Charles Leverson," said Poirot. "Until this moment, though I know the criminal, I am not sure of his name; but at last all is clear."

He stepped down the stairs and tapped the secretary on the shoulder.

"I am obliged to go to London immediately. Speak to Lady Astwell from me. Will you request her that everyone should be assembled in the Tower room this evening at nine o'clock. I shall be there then, and I shall reveal the truth. Ah me, but I am well content."

And breaking into a fantastic little dance, he skipped from the Tower room. Trefusis was left staring after him.

A few minutes later Poirot appeared in the library, demanding if anyone could supply him with a little cardboard box.

"Unfortunately, I have not such a thing

with me," he explained; "and there is something of great value that it is necessary for me to put inside."

From one of the drawers in the desk Trefusis produced a small box, and Poirot professed himself highly delighted with it.

"Just what I need," he declared.

He hurried upstairs with his treasure-trove. Meeting George on the landing he handed the box to him.

"There is something of great importance inside," he explained. "Place it, my good George, in the second drawer of my dressing-table, beside the jewel case that contains my pearl studs."

"Very good, sir," said George.

"Do not break it," said Poirot. "Be very careful; inside that box is something that will hang a criminal."

"You don't say, sir," said George.

Poirot hurried down the stairs again and, seizing his hat, departed from the house at a brisk run.

His return was more unostentatious. The faithful George, according to orders, admitted him by the side door.

"They are all in the Tower room?" inquired Poirot.

"Yes, sir."

There was a murmured interchange of a few words, and then Poirot mounted with the triumphant step of the victor to that room where the murder had taken place less than a month ago. His eyes swept round the room. They were all there: Lady Astwell, Victor Astwell, Lily Margrave, the secretary, and Parsons the butler. The latter was hovering by the door uncertainly.

"George, sir, said I should be needed here," said Parsons, as Poirot made his appearance. "I don't know if that is right, sir."

"Quite right," said Poirot. "Remain, I pray of you."

He advanced to the middle of the room.

"This has been a case of great interest," he said in a slow, reflective voice. "It is interesting, because anyone might have murdered Sir Reuben Astwell. Who inherits his money? Charles Leverson and Lady Astwell. Who was with him last that night? Lady Astwell. Who quarrelled with him violently? Again Lady Astwell."

"What are you talking about?" cried Lady Astwell. "I don't understand, I——"

"But someone else quarrelled with Sir Reuben," continued Poirot in a pensive voice. "Someone else left him that night white with rage. Supposing that Lady Astwell left her husband alive at a quarter to twelve that night, there would be ten minutes before Mr. Charles Leverson returned: ten minutes in which it would be possible for someone from the second floor to steal down and do the deed, and then return to his room again."

Victor Astwell sprang up with a cry.

"What the hell——?" He stopped, choking with rage.

"In a rage, Mr. Astwell, you once killed a man in West Africa."

"I don't believe it," cried Lily Margrave.

She came forward, her hands clenched, two bright spots of colour in her cheeks. Poirot gave her a swift glance.

"I don't believe it," repeated the girl.

She came close to Victor Astwell's side.

"It's true, Lily," said Astwell; "but there are things this man doesn't know. The fellow I killed was a witch-doctor who had just massacred fifteen children. I consider that I was justified."

Lily came up to Poirot.

"M. Poirot," she said earnestly, "you are wrong. Because a man has a sharp temper, because he breaks out and says all kinds of things, that is not any reason why he should do a murder. I know—I *know*, I tell you, that Mr. Astwell is incapable of such a thing."

Poirot looked at her, a very curious smile on his face. Then he took her hand in his and patted it gently.

"You see, Mademoiselle," he said gently, "you also have your intuitions. So you believe in Mr. Astwell, do you?"

Lily spoke quietly, albeit with a little break in her voice.

"Mr. Astwell is a good man," she said, "and—he is honest. He had nothing to do with the inside work of the Mpala goldfields. He is good through and through, and—I have promised to marry him."

Victor Astwell came to her side and took her other hand. He was quite quiet now.

"Before God, M. Poirot," he said, "I didn't kill my brother."

"I know you didn't," said Poirot.

His eyes swept round the room.

"Listen, my friends. In a hypnotic trance, Lady Astwell mentioned having seen a bulge in the curtain that night."

Everybody's eyes swept to the window.

"You mean there was a burglar concealed there?" exclaimed Victor Astwell. "My God! what a splendid solution."

"Ah!" said Poirot gently, "but it was not *that* curtain."

He wheeled round and pointed to the curtain that masked the little staircase.

"Sir Reuben used the bedroom the night prior to the crime. He breakfasted in bed, and he had Mr. Trefusis up there to give him instructions. I don't know what it was that Mr. Trefusis left in that bedroom, but there was something. When he said good night to Sir Reuben and Lady

Astwell, he remembered this thing and ran up the stairs to fetch it. I don't think either the husband or wife noticed him, for they had already begun a violent discussion. They were in the middle of this quarrel when Mr. Trefusis came down the stairs again. The things they were saying to each other were of so intimate and personal a nature, that Mr. Trefusis was placed in a very awkward position. It was clear to him that they imagined he had left the room some time ago. Fearing to arouse Sir Reuben's anger against himself, he decided to remain where he was and slip out later. He stayed there behind the curtain, and as Lady Astwell left the room, she subconsciously noticed the outline of his form there. When Lady Astwell had left the room Trefusis tried to steal out unobserved, but Sir Reuben happened to turn his head and became aware of the secretary's presence. Already in a bad temper, Sir Reuben hurled abuse at his secretary, and accused him of deliberately eavesdropping and spying.

"Messieurs and madame, I am a student of psychology. All through this case I have looked, not for the bad-tempered man or woman—for bad temper is its own safety valve, he who can bark does not bite—no; I have looked for the good-tempered man, for the man who is patient and self-controlled, for the man who for nine years has played the part of the under-dog. There is no strain so great as that which has endured for years, there is no resentment like that which accumulates slowly. For nine years Sir Reuben has bullied and browbeaten his secretary, and for nine years that man has endured in silence. But there comes a day when, at last, the strain reaches its breaking-point—*something snaps*. It was so that night. Sir Reuben sat down at his desk again, but the secretary instead of turning humbly and meekly to the door, picks up the heavy wooden club, and strikes down the man who had bullied him once too often."

He turned to Trefusis, who was staring at him as though turned to stone.

"It was so simple, your *alibi*. Mr. Ast-

well thought you were in your room, but
no one saw you go there. You were just
stealing up to bed after you had struck
down Sir Reuben, when you heard a
sound, and you hastened back to cover,
behind the curtain. You were behind
there when Charles Leverson entered the
room; you were there when Lily Margrave
came. It was not till long after that that
you crept up through a silent house to
your bedroom. Do you deny it?"

He advanced upon the quivering man.
Trefusis began to stammer.

"I—I never——"

"Ah! let us finish this. For two weeks
now I have played the comedy, I have
shown you the net closing slowly round
you. The finger-prints, the foot-prints, the
search of your room with the things
artistically replaced. I have struck terror
into you with all of this, you have lain
awake at night fearing and wondering
did you leave a finger-print in the room
or a foot-print somewhere? Again and
again you have gone over the events of
that night wondering what you have done

or left undone, and so I brought you to the state where you made a slip. I saw the fear leap into your eyes to-day when I picked up something from the stairs where you had stood hidden that night. Then I made a great parade, the little box, the entrusting of it to George, and I go out."

Poirot turned towards the door.

"George?"

"I am here, sir."

The valet came forward.

"Will you tell these ladies and gentlemen what my instructions to you were."

"I was to remain concealed in the wardrobe in your room, sir, having placed the cardboard box where you told me to. At half-past three this afternoon, sir, Mr. Trefusis entered the room, he went to the drawer, and took out the box in question."

"And in that box," continued Poirot, "was a common pin. Me, I speak always the truth. I did pick up something on the stairs this morning. That is your English saying, is it not? 'See a pin and pick it up, all the day you'll have good luck.' Me, I have had good luck, I have found the murderer."

He turned to the secretary.

"You see," he said gently, "*you betrayed yourself.*"

Suddenly Trefusis broke down. He sank into a chair sobbing, his face buried in his hands.

"I was mad," he groaned, "I was mad; but oh! my God, he badgered and bullied me beyond bearing. For years I had hated and loathed him."

"I knew," cried Lady Astwell.

She sprang forward, her face irradiated with a kind of savage triumph.

"I *knew* that man had done it."

She stood there, savage and triumphant.

"And you were right," said Poirot. "One may call things by different names, but the fact remains. Your 'intuition,' Lady Astwell, proved correct. I felicitate you."

BLACKMAN'S WOOD

BLACKMAN'S WOOD

IT was when they reached the end of the wood, which should provide the best sport of the day, that Heggs first showed signs of a curious, unbucolic disquietude. He still answered his master's remarks respectfully, but his eyes kept wandering to a long, sinister-looking belt of wood lying about a quarter of a mile away eastward. It was Ella Cartnell who first appreciated the half-mystic, half-terrified stare of those uneasy blue eyes.

"Why do you keep looking across at Blackman's Wood, Heggs?" she asked him.

He touched his hat mechanically. He was a short, cheery-faced man, in a worn velveteen coat, breeches and leggings—a man whom you would have hailed as a gamekeeper if you had met him on another planet. Sniffing restlessly about him were two good-looking Labradors. A rough-coated retriever sat by his side, wagging his tail persistently. The man was typical of his class in build, feature and speech. Yet the mystery of his eyes was the mystery of fear.

"Begging your pardon, my lady," he said, "I was just hoping that we'd keep the pheasants from flying that way. If I might make so bold, sir," he went on, turning to his master, who was standing by with half a dozen labelled sticks under his arm, "I'd like an extra gun here."

Richard Cartnell, a good-looking, large-framed young man, nodded.

"Perhaps you're right, Heggs," he acquiesced. "There's never any shooting the other side to speak of. I'll let Mr. Samson, who's walking on the left, keep well ahead and come into the ride. Then Sir John can move further down, and Mr. Johnson can come out on the meadow."

"If you'd take the corner yourself, sir," Heggs begged eagerly, "and have Mr. Morden between you and Sir John,

I think that ought to stop 'em, sir, provided there ain't much wind blowing."

Cartnell handed over the sticks.

"You can place these yourself then, Heggs," he said. "Of course, I know why you want to keep the pheasants out of Blackman's Wood, but remember this can't go on for ever. We left it alone last year because it was poor old Middleton's beat, and we haven't been in this season, but if pheasants go there, have 'em out we must. There are always woodcock round the lower end, as you know."

Again there was that curious glint in the man's eyes.

"I'll never get the beaters in there, sir," he declared.

Cartnell frowned.

"What do you mean—not get them in?" he demanded. "They're the regular lot, aren't they—mostly our own men? Surely they'll go where they're told?"

"They'll go where they're told anywhere else, sir," Heggs assented. "For beaters they're as good a lot as ever I handled. But Blackman's Wood! There's a-many as wouldn't go within a half a mile of that, day-time or night-time."

They were all three at the corner of the ride and they turned and looked at the wood below. Even in the clear, frosty light of the December afternoon, there was something grim, almost repellent, in its broken outline. Every description of tree seemed to have been planted there— tall firs, standing out stark and stiff in the middle, a medley of larches, dwarfed oaks, spruces and hollies towards the further end. Even from where they stood they could realize that the undergrowth was almost like a jungle. In a small field, at the furthest extremity, was a cottage, with a row of pheasant coops stretching away from it, and a little fenced-in garden.

"What's the idea with these fellows?" Cartnell asked moodily.

Heggs took command of himself, but there was a shiver in his voice as he spoke.

"They do say, sir," he confided, "that after Barney Middleton had strangled his wife, he made his way into the wood and hanged himself. There's some in the village who do hold by that story—old man Fouldes for one, who'd been after a few sticks, and he do swear to this moment that he saw Barney's body dangling down from a tree."

"What damned rubbish!" Cartnell exclaimed. "Everyone knows Middleton got clear away from the place. The police tracked him to Southampton."

"So us have heard, sir," Heggs acknowledged; "and though a hot-tempered man he was, for sure, I've never believed that Barney Middleton was one who would lay hands on himself. Still, there's old man Fouldes as swears he's seen his body, and many others declare they've seen his ghost. I'm not one as believes in these things myself, sir," the gamekeeper went on, "but I'd rather forfeit a week's wages than take the beaters through Blackman's Wood, even if they was willing to go."

"What do you think about it, Ella?" Cartnell asked his wife.

She turned and looked at him, without a smile on her face. She was a blonde, handsome woman, tall, and with a splendid figure. There was something inscrutable about her expression as she answered her husband's question.

"What do you think about it yourself, Dick?" she rejoined.

"I don't happen to be superstitious," he answered shortly. "I was down at the cottage this morning, and if I'd had gaiters on I think I should have tried for a woodcock in the lower end. Wherever I could see it looked terribly thick, though."

"You don't want any trouble with the beaters," Ella said. "I should try and keep the pheasants from breaking that way, if I were you.'

"Very well," Cartnell decided. "I'll do the best I can for you, Heggs. I'll come down this end myself with Mr. Morden and Mr. Johnson. I suppose we should be considered the three best shots, and I should think we ought to be able to stop them. On the other hand, if we make a mess of it, to Blackman's Wood we shall have to go. I'll talk to the beaters if you like, Heggs."

"Don't 'e say a word to them, sir, please," the man implored. "If they've any sort of a belief that they'll be asked to go through Blackman's Wood, there isn't one of them will turn up to-morrow. Don't 'e say nothing beforehand, sir, whatever 'e do."

"All right, I won't," Cartnell promised. "Anyhow, if we can keep the pheasants out, I'll forget about the woodcock and leave the wood alone this season."

Heggs touched his hat gratefully.

"It's for the sake of all concerned, sir," he said.

They strolled up the meadow to where Cartnell's two-seater car was waiting in the lane.

"It's all clear about to-morrow now, I think, Heggs," his master summarised. "We start with two partridge drives. You send your men out early, over Barrow's land, and bring in those two outlying fields of roots, and Josiah Brown's low meadows. Bring everything you can in to the rough grasses, and plan to have it done by ten o'clock. Then, unless there's a change in the wind, we'll bring them over towards Swallow Farm, and line the bottom hedge."

"There's a rare lot of birds if I can get hold of them, sir," Heggs observed.

"The second drive you know all about, but of course we must see which way the birds break."

They paused for a minute at the gate to look back. Again there was something of that curious expression in Heggs's eyes. With his ash stick he pointed downwards to the pleasant little stretch of country which they had left.

"D'you mark that, my lady?" he asked, turning to Ella. "There's pigeons coming in over Salter's Wood, and in the home spinneys yonder, and Gregory's cover, and never a one anywhere near Blackman's Wood. Just you look, sir," he went on, with a note almost of excitement in his tone. "Pigeons everywhere, and not a single one over Blackman's, though there's many of the trees there they do reckon to be fond of. Them birds knows something, they does. Sometimes they knows more than human beings."

Cartnell climbed into the car, where his wife had already seated herself.

"You go home and have a good night's rest, Heggs," he advised; "and put Blackman's Wood out of your mind."

During the whole of the drive home, Ella Cartnell sat speechless, her eyes fixed on the country ahead. As they turned in at the avenue, her husband took his pipe from his mouth and broke the silence.

"You're not tired, Ella?"

"Not in the least," she answered.

"Feeling all right?"

"Perfectly."

He looked at her in rather helpless fashion. Something had come down between them, which for months he had battled against unsuccessfully. It was there now, visible in her air of detachment, her cold aloofness, as though she were unaware even of his presence.

"What were you thinking of?" he inquired.

She turned and looked at him.

"I was wondering," she confessed,

"whether we should ever know who poor
Betty Middleton's lover was—the man
whom Barney Middleton found her with
that afternoon?"

Cartnell almost grazed a white post, as
he swung into the avenue.

"Why do you want to know?" he asked.

"It would ease my mind," she replied.

The remainder of the guests for the
morrow's shoot had arrived during the
absence of their host and hostess, and
were being served with tea by Sybil
Cartnell, Richard's young sister. Hugh
Morden, a long, lean man, with the typical
clean-shaven barrister's face, rather full
lips, and eyes of a curious grey-green
shade, was standing with his back to the
fire, a cup of tea in his hand, listening
to Cunningham's description of a public
dinner on the night before.

Sir John Cunningham, as a brief-giving
lawyer, was entitled to his attention,
which was certainly all that he did receive,
for Morden was evidently distrait. At
the entrance of his host and hostess,

however, his whole expression changed. He greeted Cartnell in the perfunctory manner of old friends who were constantly meeting, but his eyes glowed as he took Ella's hand and, bending down, whispered something in her ear. She turned away, with a little laugh.

"So sorry to be late, you people," she apologized. "I hope Sybil's been looking after you. We've been out marking the stands for to-morrow's shoot."

"Up against a superstitious gamekeeper, too," Cartnell observed. "You and I, Morden, and Johnson, too, have got to shoot our best to-morrow. Heggs tells me that if we can't keep the pheasants from going into Blackman's Wood, there'll be a riot amongst the beaters."

Freddie Samson, a pink-and-white athletic-looking young stockbroker, who had been whispering in Sybil's ear, glanced up.

"What's the trouble with Blackman's Wood?" he inquired.

"Haunted," Cartnell explained. "One old man in the village declares that he has seen Barney Middleton's body hanging there, and there are twenty or thirty who swear that they've seen his ghost on moonlight nights."

"I thought that sort of thing had died out, even in these remote districts," Morden remarked, a little satirically. "You're not going to humour the louts, I hope, Cartnell."

The latter shrugged his shoulders.

"I can't drive them in if they won't go," he pointed out. "As a matter of fact, though, unless we lose our pheasants from the big wood, and they find their way there, it won't be worth going through."

Conversation drifted into other channels. In the background of the little circle, Richard Cartnell, with a cup of tea in his hand, lounged against the corner of a table, apparently listening to a discussion upon a recent election, but in reality watching his wife and Morden. He was by nature an unsuspicious man. In their twelve years of married life, Ella had never once given him cause for serious uneasiness.

Her undoubted attraction had always brought her a train of admirers, with whom she had amused herself light-heartedly but discreetly. Morden, however, from the first, although silent in manner and secretive in his methods, had betrayed an infatuation which half surprised and half provoked his host. He watched them now gloomily. There was something about their confidential whispers, their reserves, the slightly forced smile with which Ella answered the remarks addressed to her by any of the others, which puzzled him.

They were all intimates. Jack Mason, an old friend of Ella's, a clubman who seemed to spend half his time in country houses, Sinclair Johnson, M.P. for the Division, and Jack Halloway, a nephew of the house, were all talking away of their mutual friends, and exchanging gossip as to their doings.

More and more, Ella and Morden remained outside the little circle. What the devil could the fellow be saying, Cartnell wondered, as he watched him lean closer and closer towards her. Finally, in a fit of restlessness he strolled off, with his hands in his pockets to the gun-room. He took down one of his Purdeys, to be sure that it was properly oiled, removed the lid from a fresh case of cartridges, tried to occupy himself in any way in order to regain a normal attitude of mind. When he returned to the lounge, Ella and Morden had disappeared.

"Where's Morden?" he inquired.

"Gone with Ella to the billiard-room," Sybil replied, bending forward to light a cigarette. "I say, Dick, what's the matter with Ella? She seems up in the clouds half the time. Is she having a flirtation with Hugh Morden?"

"Not that I'm aware of," her brother answered. "Perhaps," he added, with gloomy sarcasm, "even if they were, I might be just the one person whom they wouldn't take into their confidence."

"That's all very well," Sybil complained, "but I'd marked Hugh Morden down for my own. He never leaves Ella's side if he can help it. See to it, Dick, there's a dear! Separate them, and hint that there's another of the same family without a hulking husband in the way."

"Talking about Blackman's Wood," young Samson observed, throwing down an evening paper and joining them, "that gamekeeper of yours was never caught, was he, Cartnell? What was it all about, anyhow?"

"A simple, but alas! a common story," Cunningham recounted. "Middleton was supposed to have gone home towards the end of a day's shooting earlier than he was expected, and found his wife a little too pleasantly engaged with a caller. He adopted primitive measures, and strangled her."

"How sweet of him!" Sybil exclaimed. "So unlike the modern husband!"

Some impulse prompted Cartnell to turn his head. Morden and Ella had apparently been crossing the hall, and were standing now, as though transfixed, upon the edge of the circle. To Cartnell there was something terrifying about the strained look in his wife's face, an expression almost of horror in the eyes that met his. By her side Morden stood, grave and expressionless, save that there was a faintly cynical turn at the corners of his lips.

"Please don't depress us any more by talking about that horrible affair," she insisted angrily. "You've all had a longish journey—why don't we change early and have more time for cocktails? Perhaps by then you'll all think of something more cheerful to talk about. This isn't a palace, as you know, and you've only two bathrooms to scramble for."

Everyone acquiesced, and there was a prompt exodus from the hall. Cartnell, after a few minutes' reflection, went sombrely to his room, knocked at the door of his wife's apartment, and entered.

"What is it?" she asked, startled.

"Need it be anything particular?" he rejoined quietly. "I just strolled in."

"Why—of course not," she answered. "Do yo. want the bathroom?"

"Presently."

He sank into an easy-chair, and pondered for a moment or two.

"Ella," he said, "I have never inter-

fered with any of your harmless flirta-
tions—in fact, I have sometimes encouraged
them—but I cannot absolutely ignore the
fact that this change in your manner,
which I ventured to hint at the other
afternoon, all dates from this summer,
when Morden stayed down with us. Are
you falling in love with him?"

She swung round, relentlessly beautiful notwithstanding the trouble which
lurked in her eyes.

"If I am," she demanded, "do you
complain?"

"Most vehemently," he replied, "if it
is in any way the cause of your altered
demeanour towards me. Furthermore, I
don't mind telling you that I would rather
you had chosen any other friend I have
to amuse yourself with."

"And why?"

"Because," Cartnell answered deliberately, "Morden, who is a good fellow
with us men, and whom we all like and
admire because he is fiendishly clever, is
not to be trusted with a woman."

"You say that!" she murmured.

"I do," he assented. "A good many
men with attractive wives have found it
out before, and have had to have him on
the carpet. I am wondering whether that
will happen to me."

She rose to her feet and moved slowly
towards him. She was almost as tall as
he was.

"Dick," she said, "I never believed
that you were mean enough to say these
things about a man who is a guest in your
house. Why do you ask him to shoot?
Why do you have him here at all?"

"Because, my dear," he replied, "I
have always believed in the old saying—
that there is honour amongst thieves. I
know very well that Morden can't be
trusted with a woman, but that isn't my
business until it becomes my business. If
ever it should," he added, rising to his
feet, "I should know how to deal with
him."

He passed back to his room. His wife
looked after him until the door was closed.
Then she returned to her seat before the
looking-glass.

Late that night, Heggs, after he had knocked out his pipe and prepared for bed, slipped out from his cottage door, glanced up into the tops of the trees, listened, moistened his finger, and held it up in seafaring fashion.

"What are you after, John?" his wife called from the open door. "Be you thinking there's poachers about to-night?"

John Heggs shook his head.

"No fear of that," he answered. "The Sergeant's sending a couple of men round to give me a night's rest. It was just the wind."

It was a somewhat listlessly spent evening at Cawston Farms, as Cartnell's country house was called. For some reason or other, everyone was sleepy and anxious to go to bed early in view of the shoot on the following day. There was difficulty, even, in making up a rubber of bridge for Cunningham. Morden flatly refused to play, Ella also excused herself; so, eventually, Cartnell, an indifferent performer who loathed the game, was forced to cut in.

They played in the lounge, and Cartnell committed every sin known to the card tyro. He revoked, he neglected to attempt the simplest finesse, he led to no trumps as though it were a trump suit, he reduced his respective partners to tears and blasphemy. After the game was over, Cunningham walked to the sideboard and mixed himself a whisky-and-soda. For a Portland Club authority, he had kept his temper admirably.

"Dick," he advised, "get away to bed and have a long rest. No man could make such an utter idiot of himself with the cards if he hadn't something on his mind. Go and sleep it off before to-morrow."

Cartnell accepted the rebuke humbly.

"I'll just round the others up first," he observed. "I think everyone's for turning in early."

In the smoking-room he found only Jack Mason and Samson yarning, and Johnson fast asleep. He passed on to the billiard-room, opened the door, and stood for a moment upon the threshold. Morden and Ella were leaning over the billiard-table, Morden talking earnestly, his hand resting upon hers. With a swiftness which bespoke long practice, he drew his fingers away at the opening of the door. He was careful, however, not to change his position.

"Got a hiding, as I knew I should, Dick," he remarked. "No one can give Ella fifty."

Cartnell advanced further into the room. His wife turned and faced him. She was a little nervous, but his expression told her nothing.

"I think you had better go and look after your other guests, Ella," he suggested. "They are all thinking of going to bed."

He held the door open for her, and she passed out silently.

"Bed's not a bad idea. I think I'll be off, too," Morden announced with a yawn.

Cartnell, however, closed the door and stood with his back to it.

"Just one word with you, Hugh," he said. "You spoke just now of Ella having given you a hiding at billiards. Aren't you rather asking for one yourself?"

"Am I?" was the cool rejoinder. "I don't think so."

"A man's private life," Cartnell went on, "is usually disregarded by other men. I won't allude to yours, Hugh, except so far as to say that you will be a welcome guest here in the future only if you change your attitude towards my wife."

"My dear fellow!" Morden expostulated. "You don't imagine for a moment——"

"Of course I don't," Cartnell interrupted, "but that is all because I trust my wife, not you. However, wait one moment; that isn't all I have to say."

"With a man of your physique blocking the way," Morden drawled, "I hesitate to confess that I am dying for a whisky-and-soda."

"Someone," his host went on deliberately, "seems, ever since last summer, to have been poisoning my wife's mind against me. I don't know what I am supposed to have done—I can only make the vaguest guess—but I want you to understand this, Hugh. If I discover that anyone at any time has been lying to her about a particular incident concerning which I am free to admit that I have rather stifled inquiries, for certain reasons, it will not be a matter of a hiding. I shall take that man by the throat, and I shall let him go when his lips are black —you know what that means."

Hugh Morden, for a moment, had lost his equanimity.

"What incident?" he demanded. "What are you talking about?"

Cartnell opened the door.

"You know very well, Hugh," he concluded, "that I am referring to the incident of Barney Middleton's wife. Go and get your whisky-and-soda."

No more successful partridge drives had ever been organized on the Cawston shooting than the two which, on the following morning, formed the prelude to the serious business of the day. The wind had completely dropped, and, wild though a great many of the birds were, the intervening cover was so scanty that, although the drive was a long one, covey after covey dropped down in the great field of rough grass according to plan.

The seven guns lining the hedge saw the silent, flag-bearing procession of men and boys move down the hillside and slowly close in towards the boundaries of the field. There was a brief silence—then Heggs's whistle, followed by Cartnell's reply, and the beaters made their way through the hedges. A little thrill ran down the line. There was no uncertainty about this. Even the loaders—an impassive race of men as a rule—showed genuine interest in what was happening, and Cunningham, who shot but rarely, practised changing guns with his man. Then came the first warning whistle as a covey rose from just under the feet of one of the beaters, flew straight for the hedge, broke beautifully round some trees, and came over high and scattered.

The next twenty minutes was almost an epic in the history of the shoot. For once, birds, when they did swerve, left it too late, and flew high and fast down the line of the guns. Scarcely a covey went back, and just as the sport was thinning down, odd Frenchmen kept getting up one by one, flying like bullets to their melancholy but glorious end.

"Very nearly the best drive I ever had in my life," Freddie Samson declared, as he lit a cigarette and handed his gun over to his loader. "Very few runners, either. Dick, I never thought this little crowd could shoot so well. What do you think we got?"

"No idea," Cartnell replied. "I got twelve brace, and Morden was shooting beautifully. He must have got more. What did you do?"

"Ten brace and a half, and a couple of runners," Samson announced.

"Heggs has picked up one of the runners already sir," his loader put in.

"What a day for driving!" Mason exclaimed, as he strolled up. "Never had such a ten minutes that I can remember. Not a breath of wind, and they came marvellously. I never saw the crowd shoot

better, either.   That was a peach of a
right-and-left you got out of the second
covey, Dick."

They all strolled away together across
the stubble, everyone a little exhilarated.
Only the host and Hugh Morden remained
somewhat silent.   The latter's long-drawn
face seemed more than usually set.   He
smoked countless cigarettes, and kept on
a line of his own, a few yards away from
the others.   His unsociability, however,
gave rise to no comment, for everyone
knew that he talked but seldom when
shooting.   As soon as the game had been
collected and the cart loaded, Heggs
hurried up to his master.

"I've sent half the beaters round to
bring in Richards's stubbles, sir," he
announced, "and I thought if so be you
were willing to wait a bit, I'd sweep the
left-hand beaters right round to the
Orford boundary, fall in with the others,
and all come on together from the Lone
Farm.   You'll line the thirty-acre meadow
hedge, but I think you'll have to take it
a little wide, sir."

"Quite sound, Heggs," Cartnell approved. "We shan't be able to see you until you're actually in the roots, so don't forget to whistle."

The man suddenly turned his head and sniffed.

"What's the matter?" his master asked.

"Nothing, sir. I just thought—I fancied there was a breeze coming up."

Cartnell glanced at the sky.

"Might get one later on—not much sign of it at present. . . . Guns this way! We've half a mile to walk. Anyone like a lift in the game-cart? There's John with the whiskies-and-sodas and cocktails somewhere about, too."

"It's exactly an hour too early," Cunningham declared, looking at his watch. "Only one hour, mind you. We'll keep John in sight!"

The next drive, though not quite so productive, was almost as exciting as the first. Then there were three spinneys to knock out—one of which produced an unexpected show of woodcock. When they sat down to lunch on the lawn in front of Heggs's cottage, everyone was a little exultant, and good-tempered. Cunningham, who was a man of figures, produced his note-book.

"We're ahead of last year on this beat, by seventeen and a half brace of partridges, thirty-one pheasants and seven woodcock. Hares—we only got twenty-seven, did we? We're three hares short. What a morning! Ella, you and I must have a cocktail together, and, if you don't mind, Dick, I'd like to take a double one to Heggs. With only one other man who knew anything at all about the job, he brought those birds to-day as cleverly as anything I've ever seen."

Heggs accepted congratulations with a modest grin, and drained the contents of the glass offered him. They lunched at a long table set out on trestles, after Sybil, from a hastily improvised bar, had served everyone with cocktails. Hugh Morden, as usual, found a place by Ella's side. Cartnell, at the other end of the table, was as far removed as possible. To all appearance, he never glanced either towards his wife or Morden. Nevertheless, both were at times uneasily conscious of his presence. No one else appeared to notice that there was a cloud upon what was otherwise certainly a wonderful party.

After lunch came the *pièce de résistance*—the shooting of the wood. From the moment when the places were taken for the first drive—usually an unimportant one—a change came over Heggs. The effect of the extra glass of beer he had drunk at luncheon time, with a view to drowning his apprehensions, had passed. He kept looking at the sky. Already the tops of the trees in the wood were rustling. He turned to his master almost despairingly.

"There's a west wind coming up for sure, sir," he groaned. "It will carry them pheasants right away to Blackman's Wood."

Cartnell, moody and depressed himself, was unsympathetic.

"Let 'em go there, then, if they can get past Mr. Morden and me," he said. "The woodcock are worth one beat, anyway."

For a moment Heggs stood quite motionless. Again that rare expression of mysterious terror brought out the lines in his weather-beaten face. It lurked there in his eyes as he glanced furtively down towards the hated spot.

"Come along, Heggs," his master enjoined sharply. "These two first beats aren't up to much, but we'd better get them over."

The shooting began—a trifle erratic after a somewhat gay luncheon party, but soon settling down. As was always the case, the result of the first two beats was simply to drive the birds into the lower end of the wood, where the undergrowth was much thicker. The twenty or thirty that came out were satisfactorily disposed of, and certainly not half a dozen reached the dreaded shelter of Blackman's Wood. For the final beat, Heggs himself came forward to superintend the placing of the guns. He brought Sinclair Johnson down to the extreme end of the ride, almost in the meadow, in line with Cartnell and

Morden. The wind had freshened by now, and a couple of cocks, disturbed before their time, simply vol-planed down to Blackman's Wood. Heggs watched them with a groan.

"They'll come out this side, sir, whatever we do," he muttered, as he passed his master on the way back.

"Don't be a fool, Heggs," Cartnell enjoined irritably. "Keep your right well forward, and have the hedge knocked from outside."

Heggs's reply was respectful but gloomy.

"I'll do all that man can to keep they birds straight, sir," he promised.

He rejoined the beaters and blew his whistle. The familiar sound of the tapping of trees recommenced, and almost at once the pheasants began to come over. Ella had been in the ride with Mason and Samson, but as soon as the shooting started she came out into the meadow, and deliberately planted her stick a few paces behind Morden's loader. One or two pheasants broke early over Cartnell, and a woodcock, all of which he disposed of. Then, without the slightest warning, the tragedy of the day loomed up. The whistle blew continually, pheasants seemed to be rising from all parts of the wood, and practically the whole of them streamed over Morden's head, or between him and Johnson. That Morden should have missed the first one with both barrels, and have done no better with his second gun, was unusual, but comprehensible, because he had had very little shooting since luncheon, but what followed was simply amazing. Difficult or easy, high or low, overhead, to his left or to his right, Morden, the crack shot of the party, missed every bird he aimed at.

Everyone in sight looked at him in astonishment. Heggs came staggering out of the wood to see what had happened, and stood transfixed, as he watched the long line of pheasants streaming away to Blackman's Wood. Cartnell, abandoning all etiquette, moved up ten paces, and a little backwards, and continually shot the birds which sailed over Morden unscathed. Johnson, in response to a gesture from his host, did the same, but the situation was already lost. Nothing that they could do could atone altogether for the fact that Morden, in the one commanding position, seemed completely paralysed. Every vestige of colour had gone from his cheeks, and there was a savage gleam in his eyes. As one huge cock passed smoothly over his head untouched, he threw down upon the ground the gun which he had just discharged, and almost forgot to take the second which his loader was handing him.

"Anything wrong with you, Morden; are you ill?" Cartnell called out.

Morden just turned his head, and his expression was ghastly.

"I don't know," he muttered. "Change places with me, quickly."

Cartnell obeyed, bringing down a right-and-left of cock pheasants even as he took up Morden's vacated place. And then a stranger thing than ever happened. The pheasants which, with one accord, seemed to have made for Morden, made for him still, and the tragedy was once more repeated. Cartnell and Johnson missed nothing, but an odd bird now and then was all they got. Towards the end Morden suddenly threw down his gun again and held his head with both hands. Cartnell moved back behind him, and waved Johnson to come out into the field, but the mischief was done. There were a couple of hundred pheasants in Blackman's Wood, and Morden, with his hands still clasping the sides of his head, was swaying as though about to collapse. Ella leaned forward and touched him on the shoulder.

"Are you ill?" she whispered.

"I don't know," he gasped. "I don't know what's come over me. I think I'll go home—come with me."

Cartnell strolled up to him, and the two men looked one another in the eyes. Morden still seemed on the point of collapse.

"You can't go home, Hugh," Cartnell said brutally. "You put 'em into Blackman's wood, you let 'em go there—God knows why. You must shoot 'em when we fetch them out."

Morden made no reply. The refreshment cart, which Ella had sent for, came lumbering up. He stumbled towards it and helped himself to a strong brandy-and-soda. The effect was instantaneous. There was a more natural colour in his cheeks, and he regained some measure of his self-possession.

"All right," he agreed; "I'll do my best. I don't know what came over me—a liver attack, perhaps. I'm damnably sorry."

Very slowly, and like a man bent on a portentous errand, Heggs approached his master. The beaters were standing about in little groups, talking.

"Sorry Heggs, but we'll have to have those birds out of Blackman's Wood," Cartnell told him firmly. "Get it at the bottom end, and bring them this way. I'll send a couple of guns with you for the outsides. I'll place the others. We'll leave this side open. They aren't likely to come out against the wind. If they do, they'll be going home."

Heggs touched his hat. In his tone there was a note of desperation.

"I'm sorry, sir," he announced. "Them beaters, they won't go in Blackman's Wood."

"You mean that they refuse to obey orders?"

"Most on 'em, sir, and the rest ain't willing."

"And why not?" Cartnell demanded.

"It's no good beating about the bush, sir," Heggs replied, his coarse hands with the broken nails trembling as he leaned forward on his gnarled stick. "There's a dozen at least amongst 'em as can swear that they've seen Barney Middleton's ghost hanging round at the back end, just outside his cottage. They say he drownded heself somewhere, and keeps coming back to see the spot where he strangled his wife. I can't get 'em in nohow, sir."

"I'll talk to them myself," Cartnell announced.

He walked across and confronted them —a motley group, boys, youths and elderly men, in every variety of costume, but all of them wearing the leggings which had been Ella's Christmas gift.

"Look here, my men," Cartnell began, "what's this nonsense about not wanting to go into Blackman's Wood? You've seen for yourselves that the pheasants are there, and we know there are woodcock."

No one was willing to be spokesman. They shifted their feet and moved about nervously.

"Gosling, now—what about you?"

Gosling took off his hat and scratched his head.

"Mr. Cartnell, sir," he said, "I be a serious man as you know, and a man as has found religion. I don't hold with these stories of ghosts, but when there's half the village swears they've seen Barney Middleton's spirit wandering round in that there wood and round about the cottage, well, it does make one think, so to speak; and for the sake of the eight bob and beer we get for a day's beating, I'd just as soon keep out of trouble, sir. I never met a spirit yet, and I ain't anxious."

There was a little murmur of assent. One or two of the younger ones, however, laughed.

"I don't mind," a nephew of Middleton declared. "The old man wouldn't do me no harm."

"Same here," another lad joined in. "It ain't like as though it were night."

"Look here, then," Cartnell announced, "I'll give an extra five shillings to every beater who will come through Blackman's Wood. Now then, who's for the back of it?"

One by one, like sheep, they followed young Middleton. There were only five who refused, and they stood in a little group by themselves outside the wood. Heggs came up to his master with laggard footsteps. He seemed suddenly to be many years older.

"Is it your will, then, sir," he asked in a low tone, "that we go through the wood?"

"Of course it is, Heggs. Take your men along. Mr. Mason and Mr. Halloway will walk up with you. Knock the place out as well as you can, and don't forget the holly bushes."

They straggled off in a long, irregular line, and Cartnell busied himself in arranging the stands. Morden, after another brandy-and-soda, seemed to have recovered himself. He sat on his shooting-stick, his gun balanced across his knees, and his eyes fixed upon the forbidding little wood in front. The edge of it was bordered by a quantity of small black firs, but behind was a curious medley of trees of every description, and an undergrowth of bracken and rank grass, which appeared not to have been touched for years. A cock pheasant came flying out at a great height, almost before the beaters were in, and Morden brought it down with his first barrel, a crumpled mass of feathers, shot through the head.

"You're all right again now," Ella whispered. "Splendid!"

The whistle sounded continually, and pheasants began to come over. Everyone shot well, and Morden especially. The sound of the tapping of the trees grew nearer and nearer. Suddenly there was a silence. The whole line of beaters seemed to have stopped. The silence continued. Cartnell walked forward a yard or two.

"What's wrong, Heggs?" he called out.

Almost before the words were out of his mouth, there arose a chorus of wild yells, blasphemous, panic-stricken shrieks of unrestrained terror. Out from the wood, on both sides, tumbling through the hedges, running in frantic haste, came the beaters. Even when they were clear of the borders and in the meadow, they ran like madmen. Middleton's nephew, who had led the way in, fell head over heels and picked himself up, sobbing, to tear after the others.

"What the devil's the matter!" Cartnell shouted. "Heggs!"

A choked voice from somewhere in the wood:

"For the love of God stand clear, sir. Get the lady away! He's coming!"

"What's got the fellows?" Cartnell cried. "Have they all gone mad? Can anyone see anything?"

Almost at that moment the horror arrived. Crashing down the middle of the wood came some undistinguishable shape, too big for a fox, too big for a stray deer even—it was something which seemed to come in bounds, like a huge dog plunging straight ahead.

"Are you loaded, Hugh?" Cartnell asked him swiftly.

Morden made no answer. He was standing as though petrified, looking at something clear now of the trees, leaping through the bracken. It came over the low hedge and rails in its stride, and for that first moment there was not a person who saw it who was not paralysed with fear. It came like an orang-outang, six feet high, sometimes on all fours, then upright, a creature who had once been a man, with some fragments of filthy clothing and sacking still left, a great ragged beard, hair almost down his back, gaunt, deep-set horrible eyes, fingers black, patches of his body bleeding. Not for one instant did it hesitate. Clear of the wood, it went straight, like a savage animal who has marked its prey, towards Morden. It had come out on all fours, but as it approached it reared itself, and with a terrifying yell—a yell which no one ever forgot who heard it—and with great lopping springs, drew near to its cowering victim.

"Shoot!" Cartnell cried. "Shoot it, Hugh!"

Morden's gun, irresolutely lifted, wobbled in his hand. Suddenly his loader leaned past him, raised the second gun to his shoulder, and fired. For a single second the brute faltered. Then it came on again, its black, talon-like hands stretched out towards Morden, who stood there too terrified for flight, his gun, which had slipped through his nerveless fingers, lying upon the ground. At the last moment he turned and ran, ran blindly away, with a shriek of fear. His start was too late, however. He stumbled, and over he went, with his pursuer on the top of him. Cartnell had a horrible moment's view of those fingers clutching Morden's white throat, grinding their way into his windpipe, whilst Ella's shrieks filled the air.

Cartnell, who had sprung forward hurled himself upon the attacking beast. The loader seized him from behind, but

their united strength was absolutely use-
less. They might as well have tried to
move a mountain, until the last breath of
life had sobbed itself away from Morden's
lips. Then, and not till then, that grip
relaxed, and the beast rolled over, the
blood streaming from a wound in his
chest where the loader had shot him.

"My God!" Cartnell faltered, "it's a
man—it's Middleton!"

It was not until a fortnight after the
inquest and funeral that Ella Cartnell,
stretched upon a steamer-chair in mid-
ocean on her way to Kenya, broke the
silence which seemed to have been estab-
lished by mutual consent upon a certain
subject. She looked away from the sea,
and turned her head towards her husband.

"Dick," she asked, "did you know that
it was Hugh Morden who had been the
lover of Barney Middleton's wife?"

"I guessed it," he acknowledged.
"That's why I rather went out of my way
to have the matter hushed up. He was
always making some excuse to stroll down

there, and the day the thing happened, I knew that the telephone call back to the house was faked."

"And yet you said nothing to me?"

"What could I say?"

"You must have guessed what he was trying to make me believe."

"Not until the day before the shooting party," Cartnell assured her. "You see, he'd been a kind of a pal once. I couldn't believe he'd do such a dirty trick. Before that day, until then, I simply thought—I feared that you'd taken a fancy to him."

"Yet you wouldn't tell me?"

"Don't see how I could exactly."

She shivered a little. Her left hand stole underneath the rug, her fingers felt for his and clutched them convulsively.

"Men are different," she murmured.

Produced in conjunction with
The Readers Library Publishing Co. Ltd.